The King Cartel 3

Lock Down Publications
Presents
The King Cartel 3
Island Blood
A Novel by *Frank Gresham*

Lock Down Publications
P.O. Box 870494
Mesquite, Tx 75187

Visit our website at www.lockdownpublications.com

First Edition November 2015
Printed in the United States of America

Lock Down Publications
Facebook: Author Frank Gresham
Like our page on Facebook: Lock Down Publications @ www.facebook.com/lockdownpublications.ldp
Cover design and layout by: **Dynasty's Cover Me**
Book interior design by: **Shawn Walker**
Edited by: **Shawn Walker**

Dedication

To everyone from the beginning of time until the present who fought and fights for something worth fighting for. From our U.S. military, human rights activists, civil rights leaders, non-profit organizations, NAACP and every religious group that stands firm on their beliefs. All the single parents who sometimes do without just so their children can have. Even the thousands of men and women incarcerated that are legally fighting so they can reunite with their loved ones, I salute them as well.

The best fights are won with knowledge and wisdom. They may not be the most memorable, but they made a positive impact on others, with words so strong they made history because they implied that not all resolutions have to end in violence.

If you're a fan of my work, it may sound ironic but who I am as a person and what I believe in does not implement violence. My stories are just inventions of my mine for mere enjoyment. Writing is not only my passion, it's my survival kit, so I will never have to revert back to the claws of the streets.

Acknowledgments

First, I would like to give a humble thanks to God.

To my loving and supporting family and to my loyal partner, Renee Lamb. Her patience, commitment, love and belief in me has played a major part in my growth and success. Thank you very much.

And a special thanks and shout out to Ca$h and my LDP family. (We taking over). And to all the book clubs and loyal fans, thanks a million. Your support and friendship is greatly appreciated.

"Some people aren't loyal to you. They are loyal to their need of you. Once their needs change, so does their loyalty."

Prologue
Navy Island, Jamaica

A sharp pain shot through Jamerica's stomach, waking her up from a deep sleep. Her eyes sprung open, the room was dark and cool. A glint of sunlight peered through the drapes. She sat up breathing in short gasps. She placed her swollen fingers on her stomach. She was having contractions.

She was now nine months pregnant and confined in a 24' by 24' square foot bedroom with pink walls. The room was furnished with a nightstand, a dresser and a king size bed with tall posts that almost touched the stucco ceiling.

She was kidnapped eight months ago and brought to Gava's two-story mansion on Navy Island that sat secluded between Port Antonio's two harbors.

The island was once a favorite spot for tourists until Gava bought it three years ago for his wife, Maria, the sister of his deceased business partner, Sergio Dupree.

Jamerica slowly and painfully got out of bed. Her swollen feet made contact with the hardwood floor. She took baby steps toward the door and turned the knob. Her heart sped up. She couldn't believe for the first time her door was unlocked. She stood there for a moment thinking whether or not she should go for it. Then her conscious said, *Go ahead, go!* She slowly opened the door and looked around. The guards that were usually outside of her door weren't there. The long hallway was vacant. She slowly eased out of the room and the pain hit her again. So she hurled over and braced the wall as she walked down the hall.

The house was quiet, all except for a dripping faucet in the bathroom.

Jamerica made it to the top of the stair rail. She exhaled and then she slowly descended down the carpeted staircase.

Half way down the steps, the stairs made a creaky sound. Jamerica paused. She thought about going back upstairs but she thought about her unborn child. For the love of him, she had to try.

So she continued down the stairs. When she reached the bottom of the stairs, she wobbled through the foyer to the living room. The ceiling was high and the cream and jade antique living room suit complemented the room nicely. The blue linen curtains looked like ocean waves as they blew from the Caribbean breeze. The room was antique style and the silence made it appear ghostly. Jamerica was spooked. She paused for a mere second until she saw an old fashion telephone sitting on an end table. She then remembered that she'd memorized Damar's number after she wrote it down on her panties with her eyeliner when she was kidnapped, knowing that her abductors would take her phone.

She heard footsteps scurrying around upstairs. It was the guards discovering she was missing from her room. Her heart sped up, she glanced up at the stairs. Despite the pain she was in, she rushed to the phone and snatched the receiver. She heard a dial tone.

Oh, thank God, she breathed a sigh of relief.

She nervously dialed Damar's number. It rung several times before going to voicemail. She heard a door slam from upstairs, but she didn't panic. This was her first and probably last chance to reach him. She quickly dialed the number again.

"Who is this?" A voice finally asked sounding agitated.

Caught by surprise, Jamerica's heart almost stopped. She felt like she was about to hyperventilate. "Baby, it's me!" She whispered.

"Jamerica? Dis you?" Damar's voice quivered with weakness.

"Oh, my God, Damar. Yes, baby, it's me!" She wept, unaware of the guards coming down the stairs.

His voice was shaky. "Where are you?"

Luckily, Jamerica overheard the guards talking about the island. That's how she knew where she was, so her response was quick. "In Jamaica on Navy Island. Baby, please come and get me," Jamerica said before her call was disconnected.

Chapter 1

Damar was hurriedly packing his suitcase, lightly sweating while Sunja stood in his peripheral but he was completely absorbed. It was like she didn't exist to him anymore. After the phone call, Damar left her in the spa without saying a word and went straight to the room.

"I thought she was gone," Sunja said, fighting back the tears.

"I did too," Damar said and snatched his bag off of the bed and headed for the door in a hurry.

"She wants to get back with you, don't she?"

Damar stopped at the door and whipped his head at Sunja. "Are you coming or not?"

In the cab on the way to the airport, Sunja sat quietly while Damar made all the necessary phone calls. His first call was to Tom Prath, his stock broker. Damar was calling Tom to tell him he wanted to sell his stocks, ASAP. Unfortunately, the number was no longer in service and he didn't reply back to his email. That was strange because he just recently spoke to him.

So he had to go to plan B, which was to call Dub-Sac and Boo Boo to tell them to go by his mansion in Orla Vista and get his money out of the vault in the basement and take it to the stash house in Fort Myers. He let them know that he'd heard from Jamerica and he would fill them in later.

After contacting Dub and Boo Boo, he called Ricardo his Columbian connect because he needed to speak to him about some serious business. Ricardo told him to fly to Phoenix, Arizona to his private landing strip. Once that was established, he had to round up his crew, including Fresh. He would need all of them, crossing over into enemy territory.

Once on the jet heading to Georgia, Damar called Fresh to see if he killed Cassie like he was supposed to before letting him know what was going on.

He called several times and got no answer, so he left a text message. *Did you take care of that?*

Then his thoughts went back to Jamerica. He couldn't believe she was alive. So many things were going through is mind. *Is she still pregnant or did she lose the baby. How does she look now? Has she been physically abused? What am I going to do about Sunja? I love her but I love Jamerica more, plus she has my seed. But as a man, I gotta tell Sunja that I'm going after her.*

***

Miami, Florida, East 21st Street

Fresh was sitting on the bed holding his cell phone looking at the text message from Damar. He was contemplating hard on how he was going to get rid of Cassie.

Cassie was in the shower. He could hear her singing along to a pop song on her iPad. He closed his eyes and took an exasperating breath. Then he went into the kitchen and grabbed a butcher knife out of the drawer. He held it up and looked at it, *Damn I don't think in can do this.*

He then went and stood in the bathroom's doorway and watched her through the see-through shower curtain. When he saw she was about to step out, he quickly undressed and got in the bed and placed the knife under the pillow.

Cassie walked in the room, drying off as she stood at the foot of the bed. Fresh laid on his back with his hands laced behind his head. His eyes fell on her desirous body, her delicate face and her irresistible sapphire eyes. Her melons were mouthwatering ripe. Her dark tan meshed perfectly with her pink belly ring. Her pussy was shaved nice and neat, smooth like a peach. And her thighs and calves were well defined. He couldn't deny he had an overwhelming sexual craving for her.

But regardless of all of that, he knew he had to kill her or be cut out of the family business and he couldn't let that happen because he was next in line to be crowned the king.

But after looking at her sexy body, he had to fuck her one last time. He promptly threw the covers back and commenced to long stroking his dick. It grew hard as a brazil nut. "Oh, yeah, come and ride this dick, baby!" He sucked his teeth.

Cassie dropped the towel and gave him a seductive glare. Fresh's lean body and long cock were richly appealing. So she became wet without perceptible delay. She slowly advanced to the bed on her hands and knees like a prowling lioness stalking its prey. She was inches away from feasting. When she reached his succulent piece of meat, she spread his muscular thighs, lowered her head and licked his balls.

Fresh tensed up when her soft tongue coated his nuts with warm saliva, "Ohhh shiit," he moaned. Then Cassie snailed her tongue down between his cheeks and started licking his asshole. Fresh squirmed and pushed her away.

Cassie then grabbed the base of his dick and squeezed it with all of her might. She then swallowed half of him and began sucking him profusely like an un-weaned mammal.

Fresh moaned aloud when he felt the tingle in his penis down to his toes. Then a large amount of gummy cum spewed out his dick and down Cassie's throat.

Cassie could feel his legs twitch under her while she swallowed on his semen. When she relinquished Fresh, he was immobile. His breathing was thick. He felt weak and helpless like a newborn baby. His mind had almost psyched him out to start sucking on his thumb until his last conversation with Damar popped up in his head.

"Cuz, I'm sorry, man."

"Sorry ain't gonna get it. You know what you gotta do. Not that I don't trust you, cuz, but after you kill her, bring me her pretty little head."

Fresh closed his eyes and sighed. Then he slid his hand under the pillow and clutched the knife.

Now Cassie was gently licking his dick. It was hard and thick. It reminded her of a chocolate candy bar. Her pussy pulsated like a track runner's heart, so she came up and climbed on top of him and started riding him. The harder his dick got going in and out against her slimy walls was the tighter he gripped the knife.

A gentle gust of mango body wash filled Fresh's nostrils every time Cassie rocked back and forth. He wanted to taste her so bad right but a part of him wanted to just get it over with and get back to The Cartel.

Nigga, snap out of it and kill the bitch. Remember Damar, used ta gut this hoe. She don't deserve a nut. Bitch need to die. So go ahead, my nigga, stick her right there in the heart. Do it, do it now, muthafucka!"

Fresh's eyes blinked and he came back to reality. He could now hear Cassie's arousing moans that his mind had muted while his alter ego was convincing his mind to carry out the execution.

He carefully slid the knife out from under the pillow. His hand felt cemented to the handle. Cassie's eyes remained shut while she rode his dick with conviction.

Fresh fought his emotions and waited until she was about to climax. When she began to thrust harder, he slowly raised the knife to the side of her.

Chapter 2

By the time Damar's jet reached Durango, Colorado, he'd told Sunja what happened to Jamerica eight months ago. And that nothing was going to stop him from going to rescue her. Sonja was a little upset, but understood the severity of the situation. Her only concern was would their relationship end. Would he and Jamerica pick up where they left off?

"So what about us?" Sunja asked. Her face was affected by sorrow.

Damar glanced out of the window at the baby blue sky that had specks of scattered clouds in it. He was at a loss for words. This was the hardest question he'd ever been asked in his life. For once, he didn't have an answer for something. Jamerica and his baby were all he could think of at the moment. When he didn't respond, Sunja started to cry again. Damar heard the sniffles and looked at her.

"I honestly don't know. I probably won't know until I see her. That's the God's honest truth, Sunja. I can't make a decision right now, but you can. You can wait until I return from Jamaica or you can go back to Daytona."

Sunja wiped her eyes because Damar was letting her know in so many words that there was still a chance for them to be together.

She sighed. "I'll wait for you."

Damar gave her a shallow smile and pulled her into his warm embrace, then he whispered softly, "I'ma put you in a nice hotel, baby. I promise I'ma snatch you up as soon as I get back. Okay?"

"Okay," Sunja said as Damar caressed her hair.

Then his phone vibrated in his pocket. He took it out and glanced at the screen, it was Fresh. He got up and walked over to the mini bar.

"Yeah, what up?" Damar asked.

"I did it, cuzo. I killed that stanking hoe."

"Show me some proof but not what I wanted you to bring back to me. You can't do it right now, I'm in flight."

Damar knew it was too risky for Fresh to fly across state lines with a human head, besides he had no time to waste, saving Jamerica was more important.

"Okay, I can do that. I haven't dumped the body yet. I'ma send you a picture of her." Fresh replied. His voice sounded calm and emotionless.

"A'ight, that's what's up. Send it now."

Damar heard Fresh's keypad through the phone. "It's on the way, cuzo, I just sent it."

Seconds later, Damar saw the picture message appear on the screen. "Let me check it out, I'll hit cha right back." Damar ended the call and opened the message and blew the picture up to get a good look.

Cassie was sprawled out on a white linoleum floor. Her hair was wiry and her eyes were closed. She had a bloody crust around her mouth that looked like a pastry shell. Her neck and shoulders had grayish blue bruises on them.

Damar was satisfied so he erased the picture. Now with his underboss back, Damar was ready to carry on with his mission. He called Fresh right back.

"Yeah, cuzo, you get it?"

"Yeah, I got it. Bitch look good dead. But she's history now. Check this out, Fresh."

"Yeah, I'm listening."

"Jamerica's alive. She called me this morning. Gava got her in Jamaica on Navy Island."

"Dammmm!" Fresh said, in complete shock.

"You know anything about that place?" Damar asked.

"Just what I read in a National Geographic's magazine. It's a small island in Jamaica." Fresh replied.

"Okay, we're going to get her. So this the move. As soon as we get off the phone, I'ma charter a jet for you, Boo Boo and Dub to Jacksonville airport. The pilot will know your destination. I should be there in forty minutes.

"What about Taz and Oga?" Fresh asked.

"Keep them on the streets, we still gotta eat. But we'll talk more when you get here."

"That's a bet, I'm on my way as soon as I dump this trash off," Fresh said, referring to Cassie.

"Fa'sho," Damar said and ended the call.

Chapter 3
Miami Florida 12 p.m.

By noon, it was 110° degrees outside of Taz' gray Denali XL. He was glad he didn't pull out the convertible just to ride around and collect money.

So far they had collected eighty grand. Now they were headed to the warehouse to drop it off before going back out to collect more. Oga was pushing the whip while Taz sat in the passenger seat, neatly stacking money into a brief case. When he was done he closed the brief case and slid it under the seat. Then his phone rang, he grabbed it from the console and looked at the screen.

"Bumboclot! It's Fresh. I don't to want to talk to him, you answer it." Taz handed the phone to Oga.

Oga shook his head. "I don't want to speak to him either. Besides, I'm driving."

Taz sighed and went ahead and answered the phone.

"Gwan?"

"Don't *gwan me*, nigga, speak fuckin' English," Fresh snapped.

Taz cupped the phone and turned to Oga. "I hate this muda fucka." He placed the phone back to his ear. "What's up, mon?" Taz asked, trying to sound as calm as he could.

"Yo, me and Damar are about to leave the county. Boss shit, you know. He wants y'all peons to hold shit down until we get back."

"If it's a business trip? Let me speak to him."

"Nigga, if he wanted to talk to you, he would've called you himself."

Taz held his tongue. He knew Fresh was on a power trip and was trying to make him mad. But he wasn't going to give him that satisfaction. Taz smirked. "Never mind, your wish is mi command. We'll hold it down."

"Oh, and one more thing, nigga. When I get back to collect the money, it better not be a penny short or your ass will be looking for employment."

Fresh's direct threat made Taz' blood boil so high that if the doctor checked his blood pressure at that moment, he would be admitted to the hospital. But instead of going the fuck off, he took a deep breath and simply hung up.

Oga glanced over and saw the anger drawn on Taz' face. It disturbed him. "What he say?"

"It wasn't what he said, it was how he said it. But he said they were going out of the country and Damar wants us to stay here.

"Mon, don't let Fresh get to you, he wants to be like Damar," Oga said as he pushed through traffic.

"He will never be like Damar, never! Damar is a true leader." Taz stated.

Then Taz took it upon himself to call Damar. He had made up his mind, today was the last day he took orders from Fresh.

Damar answered on the second ring. "Yeah, what's up?"

"Hey, boss. I just got the message from Fresh, but that's not why I'm calling."

"Shiiit, what's on your mind?" Damar poured himself a glass of scotch.

"First, I want to say that I love working for you. I respect your leadership. But I hate your cousin with a passion. He's really tryin' mi patience and you know a man can only take so much. I hate to leave because of him, but I might have to."

"When he told me you were leaving, I asked him was it business and said I would like to speak to you myself. Why? Because I look at you like bruda. You help me and my family more than you know, so I feel obligated to help you in any way I can."

There were five seconds of silence between them. Before Damar responded. "Damn, Taz, I didn't know you felt that way toward me. I 'preciate it. I know how hard you and Oga work for The Cartel and your loyalty is solid. So before I lose you guys, I'll make some adjustments. Until then, you deal strictly with Boo Boo if I'm not available. And I apologize for the way Fresh been handling you."

Taz smiled. "Thank you, mi bruda!"

"It's all good, my nigga."

"Aha, mon. Can I ask why you leaving the states?"

Damar glanced over at Sunja, she looked sad staring out of the plane's window. He sighed and said in a low tone, "Jamerica is alive. Gava has her on Navy Island."

"Oh, mi god!" You going to get her right?"

"You damn right, and I'ma kill Gava's punk ass and anybody else that gets in my mutha fuckin' way."

"Yes! Let me go with you," Taz eagerly offered.

"Nah, my nigga, I need somebody to stay here in case we get jammed up over there. Once we get to Jamaica, I'm giving myself twenty-four hours to complete the mission. If you don't hear from me by then, you know to come bail us out some kinda way."

"Okay, boss. Gotcha."

"Cool, let me holla at Boo Boo and tell him what time his flight is leaving." Damar ended the call.

Taz felt better after talking to Damar, knowing he didn't have to deal with Fresh anymore but something still didn't sit right with Taz. His gut feeling was telling him there had to be a way he could help Damar. When he thought of something, he made a phone call. And after the phone call, he felt better.

When they finally stopped at a red light, he heard the smooth sound of Michael Jackson's *You Are Not Alone* playing in a white Camry next to him. Taz stopped thinking and looked over at the car.

"That's not a good look," he said, shaking his head at the two men in the Camry singing along with the King of Pop. They were all into it. The driver was moving his head side to side and the passenger was singing over Michael.

Oga leaned up to see what Taz was talking about. When he saw the two men singing, he burst out laughing, then the light changed and the car pulled away.

Taz looked at Oga. "Some songs two men shouldn't listen to when they're riding together."

"And that's one of them," Oga said and they both started laughing.

***

Ten minutes later…

The sleek Denali was pulling into a warehouse on 21st street. Before the garage door could close, a silver Crown Vic sped up to their bumper. They didn't realize they had company until they heard the police siren.

Whoo! Whoo!

They both turned around.

"Ah, shit! What's the date?" Oga asked as he put the truck in park.

Taz glanced at his watch and shook his head. "Damn, we late."

The driver of the Crown Victoria slowly got out and walked over to the driver's side. He leaned in the truck and propped his elbows on the door. He was a light-skinned brother with curly hair, wearing a tan jacket with blue jeans.

"You're not supposed to come here. We had an agreement," Oga said.

The man chuckled, "Well, we also agreed that you would pay me on the first of every month. Today's the fourth, so where's my shit?"

Oga's face screwed up. "We got yo money, but don't bring your ass around here no more! We don't want nobody thinking we friends because we ain't."

"Yo, mon, don't waste your breath. Let me give it to him, so he can get the fuck outa here." Taz grabbed the briefcase from under the seat. He sat it in his lap and then released the latches. The lid popped open and the man's eyes widened.

"Damn, I should charge y'all Jamaicans a fuckin' late fee."

Taz counted out ten thousand dollars and handed it to the man. "Like me bruda said, don't bring ya pussyclot ass here no more."

The man's smile went away and his nose twitched because Taz struck a nerve. He knew not to push his luck because those two Jamaicans cared more about going to jail than dying.

That's why they paid the crooked cop good every month, to keep the heat off of them and get the information they needed. So before this pay day turned into an altercation he put away his tough guy attitude, took the money and stepped away from the truck. "From now on, pay me on time." He then turned around and walked back to his car.

Oga hit the garage button over the rearview, so the Crown Vic could exit the garage. Taz hopped out of the truck with the briefcase. He went straight to the back and stashed the money in the safe. Once the money was secure, they left the warehouse to collect more debts.

An hour later…

Today turned out to be a good day for Taz and Oga. None of their street soldiers came up short. Not even a dime was missing. They collected an additional one hundred grand to add to Damar's fortune. Now they were headed back to the warehouse.

"Ayo, Taz, wanga to the strip club tonight?" Oga asked as he steered the truck through bikini land. The strip was crowded.

Taz smiled because it was like Oga read his mind. He nodded. "Yeah, mon, let's go. I got bands to make a bitch dance."

"Ha, ha, ha! No, Taz, we got bands to make a bitch leave her nigga."

When Taz started to laugh at Oga's comment, a baby blue Chevy Caprice rode up beside them at the light. The extra chrome features, growling pipes and loud music stole his attention.

"Whoa! Dats nice." He looked at the ride from bumper to bumper but his admiration of the car faded when he saw who was driving it. The name just rolled off the tip of his tongue. "Tech."

Off of impulse, Taz reached for the Glock tucked in his waist.

Oga glanced over at Taz' sudden move. "What's upa?" He asked at the same time the light turned green.

Taz yelled, "Follow that car!"

Oga didn't hesitate, he just did as his partner said. They followed him up two streets before Oga asked. "Who dat?"

Taz was reluctant to answer right away. He was too busy slamming hollow-tips into the clip. His hands were trembling. He wanted Tech badder than a hog wanted slop. When he finally filled the magazine, he grilled Oga and replied, "You remember mi runner, Coco, from Ivey lane projects?"

Oga thought for a second and then he remembered. "Oh, yeah. He was killed at McDonalds in Orlando."

Taz nodded. "Yeah, dat was him and he was good people. And dats da nigga who peeled his cap."

After a couple of blocks, Taz realized that Tech was driving in circles. "He's joy riding." Oga assumed.

"I see, just keep following him. He has to pull over sooner or later. But the way I feel, I will chase him to hell if I have to."

"Mon, you hate him that much, huh?"

"Fuckin' right! He killed mi friend in cold blood. Mi friend, Missy, was with Coco that night. She saw the whole ting." Taz thought back to how she told the story. It was so graphic it made Taz feel like he was there that night.

"We had just pulled into McDonalds on Crenshaw. It was me, Trina, Coco, Meat and Twan. Me and Trina wasn't hungry but Coco and dem was, they had been drinking and smoking weed all day. The drive thru was packed, so Coco parked and all the guys got out. A few minutes later I saw Coco put his hands in Tech's face. I couldn't hear what they were arguing about, so I let the window down.

"Coco was confronting Tech about some money he owed him. 'Where my shit, nigga, you must think this a fuckin' game.'

"By then, me and Trina had gotten out the car. Coco was all in his face. He was turnt the fuck up. I was on the sideline like a cheerleader screaming 'Yeah, fuck his ass up.'

"I should've known something was about to go down, 'cause Tech was too calm. Next thing I knew, niggas was jumping all out of cars and shit. They surrounded Coco and dem. Coco didn't back down, he was still talking cash shit and Twan was trying to calm him down.

'Chill, Coco, let dem have that little bit.' Twan was begging him, but Coco wouldn't listen. He just kept popping.

'Fuck that, ain't nobody ever took shit from me! Fuck all y'all niggas.'

"And when he said that, all hell broke loose. Niggas started shooting and Tech pulled out his gun and shot Coco right in the face. I closed my eyes and started crying. It seemed like they were never gonna stop shooting. But as soon as they stopped, I looked up, and when I saw Coco, Meat and Twan on the ground surrounded by all that blood, my whole body locked up. I almost stop breathing. It was so sad. It was the worst day of my life. I lost three friends in one night."

Missy's recount of Coco's murder had Taz sizzling inside. He began tapping his foot on the floor board, he was getting impatient. He was dying to see Tech take his last breath.

When they stopped at another red light his burning desire almost made him jump out of the truck and shoot Tech in broad daylight. But he knew he had too much at stake. It was best to stick with what he was taught back in Jamaica, which was patience, calculation, then execute. So he refrained from his irrational thoughts until the time was right.

Taz didn't know it, but it was a good thing he stayed his ass in the car because Tech noticed them trailing him two blocks ago. So he had his Glock in his lap with the safety off.

The light changed and Tech made a turn on 24th street. Oga followed him another mile until Tech pulled into a deserted plaza. There were only three cars at the liquor store, one at the laundry mat and the carwash was empty.

When Tech drove into the automatic car wash, Taz looked at Oga and smiled.

"This is going to be sweet as bear meat. Park next to that car." Taz pointed at a red Audi on the side of the laundry mat.

Oga parked. Taz concealed his Glock, threw on a baseball cap and hopped out of the vehicle. He crept alongside the brick wall and entered the exit end of the carwash. The bay was steaming hot. It didn't bother Taz one bit. He walked in unfazed and stood in front of the rinse area. He could see Tech's Chevy up ahead coated with pink soapsuds. He watched the brushes come down, spin and wash the car.

Then he slowly pulled his Glock out and tiptoed toward the car. When he got to the driver's side he opened fire. He shot several rounds through the window and door panel.

After he nearly emptied the clip, he snatched the door open. Shattered glass crumbled on his sneakers. He looked inside of the car, but there was no one there.

"Oh shit!" He knew he was fucked.

"Looking for me, muthafucka?" A voice came from behind him.

Taz raised his hands and slowly turned around. Their eyes locked. Tech recognized him off the dribble. He grinned and an old bullet wound on his right cheek stretched. "Oh, it's you. You tryna avenge your niggas?" Well, you ain't getting no points off me today, nigga. I'ma kill your ass, then I'ma go outside and kill that nigga with you. Now get on your knees and set the gun down."

"Fuck!" Taz got down on his knees and gently laid the gun on the concrete.

Tech's stocky frame walked over with a slight limp and placed the gun between his eyes. "You Jamaican piece of shit, I hate you muthafuckas."

Taz closed his eyes.

Boc! Boc! Boc! Boc!

All Taz felt was pain in his eardrums. He slowly opened his eyes and saw Tech laying to the side of him. His eyes were half closed and his mouth was moving. Then his head flopped to the side.

Taz grabbed his Glock and got to his feet. He heard footsteps and turned to the sound. He saw the silhouette of someone walking his way, through the heavy steam. He raised his gun and waited. When the person came into view, Taz sighed and lowered his gun. "How did you know to come?"

Oga tucked his gun. "Because his car was clean. Why would he wash it again?"

Taz nodded, "Yeah, mon, my calculation was wrong. He knew we were following him."

Then they looked down at Tech. "You tink he's dead? Oga asked.

He gave Oga a side stare. Then aimed his Glock down at Tech and fired two shots into his head.

Boc! Boc!

"Yeah, he's dead."

Then they calmly walked out of the carwash and back to the truck. Taz got in and took a deep breath. He felt much better knowing Coco's killer was dead and the refreshing A/C added to his delight. He turned and gave Oga a satisfied grin, then they heard police sirens.

"Oh shit! Let's go!" Taz said.

Oga hit the ignition, but the truck wouldn't start.

"What's upa?" Taz asked.

Oga looked at the gas hand. "Bomba clot! We out of gas."

They heard the sirens getting closer. Taz smacked the dash. "C'mon, baby, c'mon!"

Oga tried to start the truck again and this time he pumped the gas pedal. Nothing happened. He shook his head. "It won't start."

"Try again." Taz looked around to see which direction the sirens were coming from.

Oga wiped his sweaty palms on his pants and tried it again. This time it started.

Taz clapped. “Yes!”

Oga then quickly put the car in gear and sped off.

A mile up the road Taz pulled out his phone and called Damar. He told him that today was a good day. First, he told him that he got every dime out of the streets. Then he told him to tell Dub-Sac, to X Tech off of his hit list.

After getting off of the phone with Damar, Oga and Taz went to the mall to find something to wear for the strip club that night.

Chapter 4

Five hours later, Damar left Sunja at a hotel and he had Boo Boo wire her $10,000 to hold her until he returned from the islands.

He arrived at Ricardo's landing strip in Phoenix, Arizona in a black limo. The place was secluded by mountains. Ricardo used the strip for transporting coffee beans to several distributors across the United States, which was a cover-up for his cocaine trafficking.

When the limo driver opened the door for Damar, Ricardo and two huge Columbians were standing on both sides of him in black suits and dark shades. They were armed, he could tell. Ricardo looked just like Damar remembered. He was 6'2", paper-sack brown skin, hair was short and jet black and his goatee was solid white. His jaw was crooked, it looked like it had been broken before. His ebony eyes were beady and sunk back into his head. And his voice was deep, it matched his rich, renegade look.

"Hey, my friend, good to see you again." Ricardo shook Damar's hand.

"Good to see you, too." Damar replied.

"Alright, let's step into the warehouse," Ricardo said and all four men walked inside.

Inside there were twelve eighteen-wheelers side by side with *Columbian Café* in large print on the side of the trailers. Damar saw no other people in the building, it was quiet. All he heard was Ricardo's designer shoes clicking on the concrete until they reached his carpeted office.

The room had computers, surveillance cameras and switchboards on an L shaped table. Several chairs occupied the area and one sofa. Ricardo walked over to the coffee machine and poured himself a cup of coffee. He sipped. "Ahhh.

There's nothing like fresh, hot, Columbian coffee." He extended his cup at Damar. "Would you like a cup?"

"Nah, I'm good. But I 'preciate it."

Ricardo smiled and sat the cup down on the table. "First visit to Jamaica?"

"Yeah, first time," Damar said.

Ricardo was good at reading people. He saw the worry in Damar's face. But he didn't bring it to his attention, there were other ways of finding out what was wrong with him without really asking.

"When you get there, go to the So-Ho-style 107-room hotel in Kingston. A really nice place you'll love it."

"I don't plan on being there that long," Damar assured him.

"Um!" Ricardo raised a brow.

Damar acknowledged his curiosity.

"It's an awfully beautiful place not to." Jamaica comes from the Taino word for *Land of Springs* abounded with some of the world's finest rivers and waterfalls. You have the Martha Brae River. It's one of Jamaica's most popular tourist's attractions. Where you can glide down the river on bamboo rafts. Quite a treat. Then there's the Dunn's River falls. Very, very beautiful."

Ricardo was boring him, so he cut him off to let him know it was no vacation. "I'll keep that in mind, Ricardo, but no disrespect, I ain't going there for fun. I'm going on a mission. Somebody over there got something that belongs to me, and I'm going to take it back."

Ricardo grinned, making his crooked jaw look more deformed. "Did you say, take? That's a powerful word."

"Yeah, I said take. I'm going to spill blood on the Island," Damar said.

At that moment, Ricardo received a call on the radio.

"Base one, we're about to land," A pilot said.

Ricardo picked up his radio and pressed the side button. "Base one, copy."

Chapter 5

Minutes later, the pilot, Dub-Sac, Boo Boo, Fresh and a man Damar didn't know walked into the office. Damar greeted his crew with a *what up* and a head nod, then he looked at this new face, "Yo, is he with them or us?"

Boo Boo walked up to Damar. "He's one of my runners. Nigga on the run. He didn't have nowhere to go, so I figured we could use an extra man."

Damar then stepped to the dude. He was tall and light skinned with a full bread but Damar could still see the youth in his face. "What's your name, my nigga?"

"Mario."

Damar nodded. "That's a good name, kid. How old are you?"

"Twenty-one."

Damar then asked, "Okay, so what's you on the run for?"

Mario did a quick glance around the room before he answered the question. "I just shot at a couple of niggas, that's all." He shrugged his shoulders like it wasn't his first time doing it.

"Why you shot at 'em?" Damar asked.

They tried to sell dope on my block so I made dem niggas cash out."

"You did right 'cause they was fuckin' with my money," Damar said and turned to his crew. "I like this kid already. Now let's get this shit poppin'!"

After everyone greeted Ricardo, Fresh stepped to Damar. He had already told Dub and Boo Boo why they were flying to Jamaica on the flight over.

Fresh pulled out his phone and showed Damar a map on the screen. He knew Damar was ready to get down to business. "Here's Navy Island and here's Gava's mansion."

"How do you know that's his crib?" Damar asked.

"Because the GPS said it was the only house on the island," Fresh replied. "Once we get to Port Antonio, we'll have to travel by ferry to Navy Island between the harbors," Fresh concluded.

"What type of security does Gava have?" Damar asked, studying the map.

"Don't know. All I got was the map, but I'm pretty sure he got some," Fresh replied.

"Yeah, I know that," Damar said.

"Well, we need weapons," Big Boo Boo advised.

"Maybe we can buy some when we get over there," Dub-Sac suggested.

Ricardo stepped in. "That's what you don't want to do. Think about it. If a foreigner came to your neighborhood looking for guns, what would you think? What would you do?"

"Me, I wouldn't sell 'em shit. They might be buying them to use on me," Damar said.

"Right! That's exactly what they might think. And then all of you will probably end up in the ocean somewhere," Ricardo said.

"You're right. You got a better idea?" Damar asked.

"Of course I do. I saw this movie once. Can't remember the name of it. But there was a group of soldiers that went to an island to rescue some soldiers. They went in by helicopter at night. And we—I mean *they* got the hostages out quickly and quietly."

"And became heroes," Damar said, intrigued by the story.
"Yes and no. They received dishonorable discharges because the mission was unauthorized by their general," Ricardo said. Unbeknownst to everyone in the room, he was giving a recount of his last mission when he was in the Columbian military.

"Well, that part I ain't gotta worry about 'cause I'm my own boss. So, can you get me a chopper?" Damar asked.

"We gonna need some guns and night goggles too," Boo Boo added.

"Ha, ha, ha," Ricardo chuckled. "That can be arranged. I just got one question."

"Yeah, what's that?"

"What exactly was taken from you?"

Damar's jaws tightened and he gave Ricardo a grave look and said, "My girl."

Ricardo responded sympathetically, "Damn! Sorry, my friend. I have a chopper behind the warehouse. A Russian KA-31 with radar surveillance." He then turned to the pilot, a white guy wearing a Khaki safari short set. He had salt and pepper hair and he looked like he was in his mid-fifties. "Dennis, fuel the chopper."

"Yes, sir." Dennis left out the office.

"Now for the weapons," Ricardo said, glancing at Bruno, one of his bodyguards. The huge guard walked over to the wall by the water jug. He made Big Boo Boo look like a featherweight. His whole body was swole like the only thing he did was pump iron. He looked like he was about to bust at any moment. He took his fat hand and pulled an antler on the moose head mounted on the wall. It was a clever contraption to the hidden door on the wall.

Damar grinned. "Now that's gangsta!"

"Straight up." Fresh agreed as they followed Ricardo into the room. The lights were blindingly bright and had everybody squinting their eyes for a second. There was a nice display of guns on the walls. Some of the guns Damar and his crew never seen before.

"As you can see, I have the latest in high-tech weaponry. I even have missiles. But unfortunately, they can't fit in the helicopter.

"Okay, since we don't know what kind of firepower we gonna be up against, which weapons do you suggest we use?" Boo Boo asked.

"Ummm, good question." Ricardo looked over his weaponry. "First, tell me this. Whoever has your girl, are they expecting you?

"I don't know," Damar admitted.

"Alright, I say you go with this lightweight Glock here," Ricardo gripped the handgun. "Same issue CIA uses. It's equipped with a silencer and red beam."

"I'll take ten of 'em," Damar said.

"Where ya M-16's at and what about food?" Boo Boo asked.

"To your left, second rack. Same kind the Army uses and there's survival kits aboard."

"We'll take five M-16's," Damar said.

"And the night vision goggles are right there to your left. The smoke bombs and grenades are in the box on the floor."

"You got a bag we can put all this shit in?" Damar asked.

One of the guards retrieved a large black bag out of the closet and tossed it to Damar.

"Preciate it." Damar handed Boo Boo the bag to fill up.

"I'ight, we all set. Oh, I need four bulletproof vests." Damar rubbed his hands together.

Ricardo shook his head at Damar and looked him over.

"What up?" Damar said, looking down at the white Gucci sweat suit he still had on.

"Louis." Ricardo called out to the other guard who stood 6'8" an inch taller than Bruno, but not as brute. He had a long face and high cheek bones.

"Yes, sir," Louis responded. His voice was deep and he talked slowly.

"Get my friends here some army fatigues and four Teflon vests."

Damar nodded, "Yeah, that's what's up. Shit you got 'em all black?"

Ricardo rubbed his chin. "I'll see what I can do."

***

Phoenix, Arizona
Mariott Hotel

Sunja was sitting on the bed in a T-shirt and panties, frustrated. She felt the cramps twist in her stomach, but she was more focused on the cramp Damar had put in her heart. She had just called his phone for the tenth time and again it went to voicemail. She tossed the phone on the bed.

"Oh, God, what have I gotten myself into?" She fell back onto the bed.

Seconds later her phone rang. She rolled over and picked it up. The Caller ID said *Dad*. As bad as she needed a shoulder to cry on, her pride wouldn't let her answer the phone. Though she knew one day she would have to face the consequences of her actions and her father.

But not today. She hit ignore. Then her stomach pain hit harder and it forced her to get up and get a drink of water. Half way there, she started feeling lightheaded. She stopped before she got to the sink and grabbed her stomach and bent over. Then she vomited on the floor.

Chapter 6

Hours later, while Dennis was navigating the Russian KA-31 to Jamaica, Damar, and his crew were strategizing the rescue mission.

"Okay, we'll make the jump right here in the rainforest." Damar pointed out on the navigation system. "Here's the mansion about a quarter of a mile to the east. Once we reach the house, Boo Boo you kill the security system. Then we're going in, in pairs. Me and Fresh will play the front. We're gonna search every inch of that place until I find Jamerica. And after I get her, I'm going for Gava."

Damar then glanced at his watch. "We'll be in Miami in an hour to refuel. So we should make it to Jamaica around ten o'clock tonight." After everyone nodded Damar added, "Everybody remember how Dennis showed us how to use the parachutes?" Damar got a second head nod from his crew.

"A'ight, now let's lock and load. Get some rest and pray if you need too. "And enjoy the flight," Damar loaded his weapons.

***

By nightfall, the helicopter was flying along the calm Caribbean waters off of Jamaica's coast.

In deep meditation, Damar gazed out of the window not really noticing the silhouette of the Blue Mountains, the mangroves or the white sand beaches of the coastline that made Jamaica a tropical paradise.

His thoughts were on Jamerica. He was so nervous and anxious he kept checking his magazine.

He glanced over at his crew. Dub-Sac had redemption etched across his face. He was rocking back and forth, mumbling to himself. "Here we come, you muthafuckers." Despite

Dub's drug use, Damar always felt the presence of his loyalty and he loved him for that.

He looked over at Boo Boo. He was laying down with his head propped on his backpack, eyes closed, hands interlocked on his stomach. He wasn't sleeping. He was praying for a successful mission and a safe return home. Damar really didn't know Mario, the new guy, but he looked relaxed.

He then looked over at Fresh. They made eye contact. A silent pause. Then Fresh threw up his thumbs and nodded. This was his way of letting Damar know he still had his front and his back like always.

***

"A hundred yards before we reach the Harbor!" Dennis yelled from the cockpit.

"Alright, my niggas, lets tighten up. It's that time!" Damar grabbed his backpack and put his night vision goggles on. His crew followed suit.

When they reached the harbor, Dennis hovered the helicopter over the forest. He hit the door switch and the door slid open, the sea breeze quickly circulated through the aircraft. Their fatigues blew rapidly in the wind. Damar's heart sped up, his throat was dry and his skin felt clammy.

"Here's your jump spot. I'll be back in two and a half hours. Be here because I don't have a lot of fuel to be flying around all night." Dennis yelled over the noise of the propellers.

"We'll be here. You just make sure you bring your ass back to get us." Damar then crossed his heart and jumped out of the helicopter.

Fresh stepped up next. "I'm right behind you, cuzo." He jumped.

Before Dub-Sac jumped, he pulled a small bag of coke out of his pocket. He took his pinky finger and fed it to his nostrils. Once the drain hit his throat, he exhaled and plunged out of the chopper.

Boo Boo inched up to the ledge next and said, "Lord, please have mercy on me."

Then Mario walked up to the door and took a deep breath and jumped.

As Damar fell from the violet colored sky, he felt an adrenaline rush like he'd never felt before. Jumping out of a moving car couldn't compare. When they each got 300 yards from the ground they all pulled their rip cords and gently glided to the forest's floor.

Chapter 7

After twelve long hours of labor, Jamerica was finally resting. She was cradling her 7 lbs. of pride and joy. As she breast fed, she rubbed her baby's hair affectionately. He looked just like Damar but lighter. She could tell by his cuticles that he was going to be dark skin just like his father, though. Though Jamerica was overjoyed and thankful, her smile was barely visible.

She thought about the brief conversation with Damar before the guard snatched the phone out of her hand earlier that morning. There was not a day that went by that she didn't think about Damar. The first few months, she was stressing so bad she stopped eating and got dehydrated. When Gava's in-house physician ran test on her, they found out that she was pregnant.

So Gava attempted to sell her to a friend of his who lived in Montego Bay. But his wife, Marie, who didn't like Jamerica at first because she was young and beautiful, stopped him from selling her.

She wanted Jamerica to have the baby there, plus she had all the baby accessories, she bought two years ago when she was pregnant with Gava's child. Unfortunately, she had a miscarriage at five months. But she never got rid of the baby stuff in hopes of having another baby someday.

So Marie befriended Jamerica and became her confidante. She made Jamerica feel secure and protected. She gave Jamerica anything she wanted aside from her freedom, which she said Gava would give her once the baby was old enough to travel. So that part of the situation cheered her up a little and a smile of hope appeared on her face.

Then Marie came in the room all jubilant like a kid at a carnival. Marie was tall and slender, her skin tone was camel brown, her hair was long and black and she was wearing a white gown that hung over her white sandals.

"Aww, he looks so adorable. Can I hold him?" She took the baby from Jamerica. She held little Prince up and smiled at him. He had milk around his tiny mouth. His eyelids fluttered. "You're so handsome, yes you are," Marie said before suffocating him with kisses. He started to cry.

Jamerica's motherly instincts kicked in. She reached out for him. "Give him to me."

But Marie wouldn't give him up. She tried cradling him, it didn't work. He cried harder. "What's wrong with him?" Marie said out of frustration.

"He wants me, now give me my baby back." Jamerica hopped out of bed and took baby Prince from Marie. Instantly he stopped crying and Jamerica got back in bed and popped her breast back in his mouth.

Marie stood poised like a mannequin with a bitter look on her face. At that moment, Gava walked in the room unannounced. He was 5'5" and scrawny. He had a narrow face and long thick dreads. Despite his physical attributes his name spoke volumes on the island of Jamaica. He was a Ghetto Don in the people's eyes like Christopher "Dudus" Coke. Revered by the poor as a Robin Hood figure.

Gava took care of the poor and obtained their political votes. In return, the government supplied him with protection and a flow of money as well as narcotics and firearms for his loyalty in getting the people to vote for them.

He touched Marie's shoulder, it startled her. "Oh, Gava!" her arms fell to her side.

"What's upa, gyal?" he asked with a scruffy voice.

Marie leaned over and whispered, "That ungrateful bitch don't want me to hold the baby."

"You wanted her to stay, she's your problem now. Say wanga go to Dunn's River Falls tomorrow?"

The Dunn River Falls was one of Jamaica's most famous natural attractions because the sparkling waters tumbled over rocks and limestone ledges into the sea. Gava and Marie went there once a month to explore and climb the natural tiers to the top of the falls.

"Ahhh, that's a great idea. We need to celebrate anyway." Marie stared at Jamerica cynically.

When Jamerica glanced up, Marie quickly shot her a fake smile and a girly wave.

Jamerica didn't respond, she just pulled baby Prince closer to her.

"Okay, I see that you want to be alone, so we're going to bed now," Marie said.

"Hold on, I have someting fa de' gyal." Gava pulled out a satin bag. He poured the contents in his hand.

It was a silver collar with tiny bells all around it. The bells made a ringing metallic sound. Jamerica was confused.

He walked over and slipped it around her neck and fastened it. Then he took a key and locked it. "Aha, just in case you wanna run off again."

Jamerica tugged at it and it jingled. "I don't like it, take it off." Jamerica screamed.

Gava thought about back handing her, just like he used to do when she first got there. She used to fight every day and she kept trying to run away, which got her several black eyes and busted lips until her attitude adjusted. When he finally broke her, he had his way with her in more ways than one. But right now it was obvious that she'd forgotten all about them old licks upside the head. So he decided to refresh her memory. He raised his hand and drew back to strike her.

"Leave her alone!" Marie yelled.

Gava put his hand down and walked angrily out the room.

Marie went over to Jamerica. "I'm sorry, give me two weeks and I'll get you back home."

Jamerica's eyes widened. "For real?"

Marie smiled. "Yes, I promised." Then she walked out the room.

Gava was standing outside of the door. He gave Marie a suspicious look when she closed the door shut. "Why you always defending her?"

"I have my reasons. I was just waiting on her to have the baby. Now that he's here, she's useless."

"So I can sell her now?"

Marie conveyed a sardonic grin. "No. In the morning, I want you to kill her."

"What about the baby?" Gava asked in a low tone.

"He's mine." Marie walked away.

Gava smiled and whispered through the door, "Sweet dreams, mi gyal."

Not knowing that Jamerica was at the door holding the bell collar steady so it wouldn't ring. But at her detriment, she only heard the last thing Marie said about baby Prince being hers.

Chapter 8

As Damar and his crew tread through the marsh forest, they were being watched by the unseen and entertained by the night monkeys, trapezing from tree to tree. The only sounds that were familiar in the foreign place were the tree frogs bellowing and the crickets chirping. When they first landed on solid ground, Damar saw a Kling Kling black bird atop a tree and thought it was a crow until it made a whistling sound. And he had never known a crow to whistle. Along the way, Big Boo Boo found a water snake laying on a tree trunk. He caught it behind the head and put it in the satchel across his shoulder.

Damar was determined to get through the grassy vegetation. Everyone was keeping up with him except Big Boo Boo. He was way behind. His 350 lbs. was fighting against gravity as he strained to lift each leg up out of the muddy ground.

"Hold up!" he yelled out of breath and leaned up against a tree. Damar turned around and lead the others twenty yards back to Boo Boo.

"What's up, bruh, you alright?" Dub-Sac touched Boo Boo's shoulder.

Boo Boo shook his head. "Hell naw, I ain't alright." He was trying to catch his breath.

"Here, drink this," Fresh handed him a water canteen.

Boo Boo took the water and chugged it. "Ahhh, okay I'm good now. Just give me a minute."

While Boo Boo was recuperating, Damar was watchful of everything that moved with his night vision goggles, listening to every twig break and tree crack. He didn't want to be ambushed by a bunch of monkeys.

Dub-Sac stepped too Boo Boo and whispered, "Hey, my nigga, try a line of dis coke, give them legs a get right." Suddenly, there was a big splash a couple yards over in the swamp.

Splash!

What the fuck? Damar wondered.

Then a twenty foot crocodile emerged from the water. Before anyone could react the croc clamped its powerful jaws around Mario's legs. All that was heard was bone crushing screams. "Aha! Aha! Aha!"

Boo ran up on the huge reptile and aimed his gun. The animal swung its tail and knocked Boo Boo to the ground.

Fresh and Dub started shooting at its thick hide. But the croc kept shaking Mario ferociously until he ripped his body in half.

Damar ran up on the croc with both Glocks and emptied the clips into his head.

Boc! Boc! Boc! Boc!

The crocodile dropped dead with the lower half of Mario's body in his mouth.

Damar exhaled and lowered his smoking gun. He looked down at what was left of Mario. Then he looked at his crew, just like him, none of them were affected by the gruesome killing of the young man. They didn't know him long enough to be saddened by his death.

Boo Boo was just getting to his feet.

"Let's try to stay together. We don't know what else is out here." Damar looked around the dark forest.

"We got two hours left to get there and back, cuzo," Fresh said, glancing at his watch.

"A'ight, let's move," Damar said. "Come on, Boo Boo." Then he put his hand on his shoulder and they proceeded through the forest.

Twenty minutes later, Damar and his boys reached Gava's back yard. Camouflaged by a high bush. No guards were visible, at least not on the outside. Only an abundance of palm trees, flower beds and a white Gazebo.

"I see some motion lights," Damar said, scanning the property on one knee.

"Yeah, I see." Big Boo Boo took the snake from his bag. He stood up and slung it as close as he could to the house.

When the serpent hit the ground and slithered across the lawn the motion lights instantly came on. A minute later, a bulky black man walked out onto the patio. He was armed with a semi-automatic rifle. His attire was all white. He stepped off the patio and surveyed the yard. He saw something moving in the grass and calmly walked up to it. The snake quickly changed directions when it saw the man's shadow.

"Aha! Run, mudafucka!" He then went back toward the house.

Once the man was back inside, Damar made his move. "Let's go. We got a minute before the censors reset." Damar assumed.

They all crawled low and followed Boo Boo as he trailed the alarm wire to the main circuit box. He used a screw driver to open it and then he snipped the wires.

Damar then looked at his watch. "We got about an hour and a half left. We need to move."

Hold on I'ma have us in, just a sec." Boo Boo retrieved a tool to pick the lock to the patio door. Once inside, they followed the wall that led into the kitchen. At 1 a.m., Damar assumed everyone was asleep except for the guard or guards. He didn't know if he was the only one.

It was quiet and cool. They could smell the herbs and spices from the dish on the stove. When they entered the dining area, they heard footsteps.

"Quick, hit the light!" Damar whispered.

Fresh hit the light switch on the wall. Then they crouched down behind the dining table. It was another guard. This one looked Puerto Rican. He was short and muscular with a ponytail to the middle of his back. Dub-Sac forgot to close the door and the breeze was coming through the house. The guard walked right passed them and locked the door.

When he walked back through the dining room, Boo Boo jumped him. He held him in a chokehold from behind. The man's arms peddled the air as he tried to breathe.

Damar stepped to him and grabbed his knife and put it to the man's eyeball. "How many guards?"

When the man refused to respond, Damar poked his eye out with the knife. Boo Boo quickly covered his mouth and the guard's blood poured down Boo Boo's hands.

"How many muthafucka? Show me with your fingers or I'ma poke the other one." Damar hissed.

The guard was turning blue but managed to hold up two fingers.

"Just you and another one?" Damar asked.

The guard nodded *yes.*

Damar got face to face with him, "Muthafucka, who the fuck I look like? You mean to tell me that Gava got two guards on duty?"

"Yes, just two guards on the weekend." The man said once his mouth was released.

"So where's his army?" Damar asked.

"Aha! They're here on the island."

"Okay, now where's the American girl that Gava kidnapped?"

The guard looked up with his one good eye.

"Okay, who else is up besides you and the other guard?" Damar asked.

The man shook his head as if to answer *nobody*.

"Let him go, Boo Boo." Damar ordered. The man dropped to his knees. Dub-Sac quickly disarmed him.

"Get your bitch ass up and take me to her." Damar barked.

The guard slowly stood feeling for his missing eye.

"I'ight, muthafucka, lead the way. And if you even fart and I smell it, I'ma dome call your bitch ass. Now get ta stepping!"

***

"Oh yeah, gyal. Oh yeah, gyal!" Gava moaned while Maria was sucking his dick. Then he glanced at his surveillance monitors on the wall. "Bumboclot, pussy mudafuckas!" He yelled and pushed Maria to the side. On the screen, he saw four masked men in fatigues scaling the staircase. He quickly jumped out of bed and put on a pair of jeans.

Maria sat up in bed and tossed her hair to the back. "What is it?" She became frightened.

Gava turned to her before going out the door. "Get up under the bed, we have visitors. I'm 'bout to give dem a warm greeting." Gava left the room and locked the door behind him.

Chapter 9

When they topped the stairs. The other guard was six feet away, close enough to see that his partner had lost an eye. "Bomba clot!" He fumbled for his gun.

Damar threw the red-beam on him and fired two silent shots into his chest. The guard dropped dead.

"Which door?" Damar asked the guard.

Boo Boo yanked his collar. "You heard him, which door?"

The guard walked up the hall and stopped at the third door to the right.

"Is she in here?" Damar asked anxiously.

The guard nodded still holding his head.

Damar looked at everyone and took a deep breath. He then went into the room. It was dim, but he could see Jamerica lying in bed. He slowly walked over and stood by her. She had on a white night gown. She was still beautiful to him, just a little pale. He sat down on the bed and whispered her name. "Jamerica. Jamerica."

When she opened her eyes and saw him, she smiled. "I miss you, baby, I wish you was here." She thought she was dreaming.

Damar smiled and wiped a tear from his eye. He leaned down and kissed her. That's when she realized he was real and wrapped her arms around his neck and started planting kisses all over his face. "Oh, Damar. Oh, my king. You're here, oh Damar." She sobbed.

Damar held on to Jamerica and whispered in her ear, "I finally found you." After a moment, he broke the embrace and rubbed her stomach. "What happened to my baby?" He frowned.

Jamerica then peeled the sheets back. Baby Prince was laying on his stomach. "I named him Prince Mario King."

Damar reached down and picked him up.

"Cuzo!" Fresh stood in the doorway pointing at his watch.

"Shit the choppa." Damar handed Jamerica the baby. "Can you walk?"

"Yes." She responded.

Damar looked around the room. "You got something to put on?"

"Yes, in the closet." Jamerica pointed to the door.

He ran over to the closet and opened it. There were only dresses hanging up. He snatched one off of the hanger and handed it to her. As fast she could, she slipped the dress over her gown. Then she wrapped baby Prince up in a blanket. While she was moving around, the bell collar was jingling.

Damar tried to take it off her neck, but he couldn't. "Yo, Boo Boo, take this shit off her neck."

Boo Boo came over and broke it off with his brute strength. Then Damar took ahold of Jamerica and turned to the guard." How many people left in the house?"

Boo Boo came over and applied pressure on his shoulder for not responding quickly enough.

"Ahhh," the guard frowned. "It's just Gava, his wife, two maids and a butler," he confessed.

"Alright, take us to the maids and butlers' room," Damar said.

The guard led them down the hall to the rooms. Damar's crew tied and gagged the maids first. Then they did the same to the butler. Next the guard took them to Gava's room. The double doors were locked.

"Boo Boo, take care of the door," Damar said.

Boo Boo then kicked the doors in and Damar led his crew inside.

The room was spacious, everything in it was big. The dressers, the chairs, and the bed, which was high with a white veil canopy around it and a step stool to the side. The walls were white and the carpet was thick and green. It looked like Bermuda grass.

Damar slowly pulled his Glock out and walked over to the bed. He then slid the canopy curtain over. The bed was empty.

Fresh held movement under the bed. He snug Damar and mouthed, "The bed."

Damar cocked his Glock. "Whoever's under the bed, you got five seconds to come out or I'ma shoot this mutha fucka up."

In less than two seconds, Marie rounded her ass out from under the bed and stood up. Her eyes widened, as she held her breath.

"What are you doing here? What do you want?" She asked hysterically before she screamed out her husband's name. "Gava, Gava!"

Jamerica stepped up so Marie could see her. Then she handed the baby to Damar.

"Oh, Jamerica! What's going on? Who are these people?" Marie asked, looking at Damar and his crew as she covered her cleavage.

"Dis my baby daddy, bitch." Jamerica slapped the shit out of Maria.

Maria grabbed her face and sobbed. "Why did you do that?" I'm your friend. I've always treated you good. I'm not the bad guy, he's the bad guy. Remember I promised to help you. You're like a daughter to me, Jamerica."

Jamerica looked her dead in her face. "Bitch, please!" Then punched Marie in the nose.

Pop!

Marie screamed and grabbed her nose as the blood percolated between her fingers. Then Damar handed baby Prince back to Jamerica.

“Now where’s Gava, bitch?’ Damar asked with his gun to her head.

“Rude boy! Me right backa yah!”

Everyone turned around. Gava was standing in the doorway strapped with a machine gun.

Chapter 10

"Drop your guns." Gava said, clutching the wood stock.

Nobody moved.

Damar knew one of them could take him, but that was a risk he wasn't going to take with Jamerica and the baby in the room. He moved Jamerica behind him and told his crew to drop their weapons.

They did as Damar instructed.

"Hands up," Gava said, as he sidestepped around them to get to his bed.

The guard walked over to Gava holding his eye. "Ahhh, let me see your eye," Gava said with a concerned look on his face. The guard removed his hand away from his face. Gava examined the wound, his eye was definitely out. "Don't worry, mi bruda, I will fix it. Then he gunned the guard down and chuckled, "What good is a one eyed watchy?" He turned to Damar. "You had to come for de baby 'cause your gyal's pussy is bullshit. Me like tight grip."

Damar flinched, he felt his blood surge through his body. He gritted his teeth and his nose flared out.

Jamerica's eyes were filled with sadness and hatred. She remembered those nights when Gava snuck into her room and forced her to have sex with him.

Marie gasped and jumped out of bed and ran up in Gava's face. "You been fucking this black bitch?" She yelled as she pointed in Jamerica's direction.

"Yeah, me the bad guy. Ain't dat what cha told them a minute ago?" Gava said, looking at his wife with disgust.

"What was I supposed to say? He had a gun in my face."

"Shut up and get the baby," Gava said.

Marie rushed over and reached for baby Prince. Jamerica turned her back to her. "Give him to me!" Marie yelled.

Damar winked at Big Boo Boo.

Big Boo Boo swiftly charged Gava, his wide body shielded everyone from Gava's bullets as they slammed into his Teflon vest.

Two bullets ripped through his left hand and forearm before he grabbed the gun out of Gava's hand. Then he pushed him to the floor.

Marie stepped away from Jamerica.

"Hold my baby," Jamerica handed him to Fresh. "I'm 'bout to whoop this bitch's ass." She walked up on Marie and pushed her on the bed. Then she got on top of her and started punching her in the face. While Jamerica was giving Marie a well-deserved ass whipping, Damar was standing over Gava. Boo Boo was wrapping his wounds with a torn piece of sheet.

"I told you I was coming for yo bitch ass." Damar reminded Gava. Then he glanced over at Marie when he heard her screaming and begging for Jamerica to stop hitting her.

Jamerica let up only to drag her off of the bed by her hair, then she started kicking her in the face with the flat heels she had on. "You thought you were going to take my son, bitch!" Blood splattered on the carpet each time she landed a kick. After the tenth kick to the head, Marie was unconscious, but Jamerica kept stomping her into the floor.

"Damn, rude boy, you gonna let her kill mi wife?" Gava asked with a sharp contortion on his face, not knowing that Marie was already dead.

"Nigga, shut the fuck up!" Damar yelled and kicked Gava in the mouth and he fell back on his elbows. "You must think I'ma let you live. Dub-Sac, take this nigga's clothes off."

Gava tried to resist, but Dub-Sac pistol whipped him. Gava fell limp, then Dub-Sac ripped his clothes off.

"Now hold him still. Yo, Jamerica, come here," Damar said.

Fresh was cradling baby Prince trying to stop him from crying. "Shhh, lil cuz, it's gonna be alright. Mama ain't going nowhere."

Jamerica walked over holding her stomach breathing heavy. She was in pain, she knew she had no business fighting right after giving birth, but she could've just had triplets and she was still going to beat the snot out of Marie's two-faced ass.

Damar pulled his knife from his side pocket and handed it to her. "Lift him up," Damar told Dub-Sac.

Gava started yelling and kicking. Boo Boo came over and secured his legs. They had him suspended in the air, sideways. Jamerica walked up and grabbed Gava's dick. "This time you don't have to force me to touch you." She pulled his dick and began cutting it with the ridge end of the knife. Gava screamed and tried his best to break free from Boo Boo and Dub-Sac's grip. His face crunched up like an aluminum can. When Jamerica finally finished, she shoved his dick in his mouth. "Suck your own dick, muthafucka!" Then Damar karate chopped him in the throat and he started choking on his dick. Jamerica then went over to get her baby from Fresh.

Fresh looked at his watch they had thirty minutes. "Yo Damar! Damar!" Fresh yelled. But he was so engulfed in watching Gava die he didn't hear him.

"Shiitt!" Fresh mumbled and marched over and emptied his clip into Gava's body, then he looked at Damar. "Cuz! We gotta go! We got thirty minutes."

Damar nodded and motioned for Dub and Boo Boo to lead the way. As soon as they made it to the hallway, it sounded like a stampede of cattle were busting through the front door. Dub-Sac looked over the rail and as soon as he did he was shot at. The bullet whizzed by his head and went into the wall. Dub hug the wall, while everyone else crouched down.

Damar quickly ushered Jamerica and the baby in to a nearby room and closed the door. Then he snatched his two Glocks out of his waistband.

"Fuck I knew this shit was too easy." Damar eased up to the rail and stole a grimace.

He saw a row of soldiers standing at the bottom of the steps. When they saw him, they started shooting. Damar ducked the raining bullets and put his back up against the wall and covered his head with his arms. He was still holding his guns as pieces of sheet rock crumbled on top of him. He looked over at his crew, everyone was crouched down with guns in hand. Damar yelled "Yo! y'all follow my lead. We finna get the fuck outta here one way or another."

Then Damar sprung to his feet and kissed both Glocks and ran to the rail. When he looked over, there were about twenty soldiers running up the stairs. From the incline, Damar aimed and fired away.

Boc! Boc! Boc!

His crew came up and stood on the side of him and started shooting. One by one, the soldiers in the front dropped and round down the steps. A few men in the back was able to let off some shots. It was an all-out war. The floor stairs and walls were all filled with holes. Wood pieces and dust was flying everywhere. Damar and his crew stop shooting when they saw the last man drop.

When the smoke cleared, they were able to see the bodies sprawled out on the stairs. It became silent and Damar looked at his crew. He then held up his smoking guns. "I think we got them all."

Boc! Boc! Boc! Boc!

Damar crew watched as his body shook in place. He had a shocked look on his face, his eyes and mouth were open. His guns slowly slipped out of his hands and dropped to the floor.

A soldier was standing at the bottom of the stairs shooting. Damar's crew didn't hesitate to return fire. The man dropped and rolled to the side of the stairs.

Dub-Sac then ran down the stairs and turned the corner with his gun aimed at the floor. The man was gone. All Dub-Sac saw was a spot of blood on the floor. "Mutha fucka!" Dub yelled and smacked the wall with the palm of his hand. Then he ran back upstairs to check on Damar. When he reached the top, Boo Boo had just ripped Damar's shirt open.

Jamerica crack the door open when she didn't hear anymore gun fire. When she saw Damar laying down on the ground, she ran over holding baby Prince in her arms. When she looked down and saw his eyes were closed, she started screaming. "No Damar! Nooo!" Baby Prince started crying because his mother's was screaming over him.

Fresh kneeled down and pulled her up, while Boo Boo ran his hands over the vest.

Jamerica yelled, "Say something, Boo Boo. Is he dead?"

Boo Boo couldn't reply, he was just as scared as she was. His hands were shaking. "I don't know, Jamerica. I don't know." He shook his head, "He aint bleeding. I don't see no blood."

Then Damar's head rolled to the side.

"He's moving, he's moving." Boo Boo lifted his head. "Wake, my nigga. Shake that shit off."

Damar moaned as his eyes slowly opened. He uttered the first name that came to his mind.

"Jamerica." Then he growled and forced himself to sit up.

Jamerica broke from Fresh's embrace and ran over to him. "I'm right here, baby," she said just as Boo Boo was lifting Damar to his feet.

Damar stumbled a little and rubbed his chest. "Aha! Fuck that shit hurt like a muthafucka."

Boo Boo exhaled and wiped his forehead because the bullet proof vest saved Damar's life.

When Damar saw the blood soak clothe wrapped around Boo Boo's arm, he forgot about himself. "Man. you bleeding like a hog."

Boo Bo looked down at his arm and nodded. "Yeah, I see, but I'm good."

Damar then wrapped his arms around Jamerica. He held her tightly because he thought he lost her again.

Fresh looked at Dub-Sac. "Did we get him?"

Dub shook his head. "Hell nah, muthafucka got away."

"Shit!" Fresh then looked at his watch. "Oh fuck! Yo, Damar, we got less than twenty minutes."

Then they heard a truck crank up and spin off. Boo Boo looked at Damar. "Yo, he's gon' to get help."

Damar nodded, "I know let's go out the back door." Then he led everyone down the stairs, as they all stepped over bodies they kept their guns drawn in case of another attack.

Chapter 11

When Damar got to the back door, he thought about the journey through the forest. Jamerica wasn't in any condition to walk a quarter mile right after giving birth.

"Yo somebody gotta bring the choppa back," Damar said with his arm around Jamerica's waist.

"I'll go!" Dub volunteered.

"No, I'm faster. I'll go," Fresh said.

"You sure, you got this?" Damar asked.

Fresh nodded. "Cuz, I got it." He then removed his backpack to lighten his travel. He put his Glock in his waistline, then he gave Damar a firm handshake. "Don't worry, I'll make it." Then he sprinted toward the woods. He made it to the drop spot in exactly twenty-two minutes, then he struck a striker into the air.

In less than four minutes, the helicopter was hovering above Fresh. He waved at the chopper as the blades generated a swirl of wind around him. A ladder dropped and Fresh grabbed hold of it and climbed the parallel rungs until he reached the top. Once inside of the chopper, he slid the door closed and walked up to the pilot.

"We gotta go back and get them, hurry," he said out of breath.

Dennis quickly pulled a lever and the chopper went horizontal, toward the east.

***

Minutes Later…

"He made it!" Damar said, with exasperation as he heard the Russian KA-31 in the airwaves. When the chopper cleared the trees, Fresh could see Damar and the crew cliqued up on the patio.

"That's them, they got a baby with 'em. You're gonna have to land," Fresh said over the pilot's shoulder. Dennis nodded and turned the tail rotor.

Suddenly, a swarm of dune buggies came into view on the dirt road about two hundred yards west of the mansion. Everyone spotted them about the same time. They were moving fast. It was dark, but you could see the dust flying around the headlights. The tires crushing over the sand and pebbles. Men hollering like hoodlums on the buggies. Jamerica covered baby Prince's head, shielding him from the noise coming from both directions. It quickly became an intense moment for Damar. He yelled over the noise.

"Dub and Boo Boo, cover me. We gotta get Jamerica on first!"

Boo Boo and Dub-Sac faced the oncoming vehicles with their guns.

The helicopter descended toward the ground with the buggies less than a hundred yards away. At that moment, something clicked in Fresh's mind. *Why am I risking my life to save him and his girl when he's the one that betrayed me? This is the perfect time to get my revenge and become King of the throne. I'm not worried about him surviving this, especially when those Jamaicans find out Gava's been murdered.*

The dune buggies were getting closer by the second, Damar could smell the dust in the night's air.

When the helicopter lowered ten feet from the ground, Fresh told Dennis to lift the chopper.

"No, I can make it," Dennis yelled.

Fresh then drew his Glock and put it to the back of his head. "I said lift it!"

Damar made eye contact with Fresh. He saw Fresh pointing the gun at Dennis and the angry silence drawn on his face just before the chopper flew away.

"Damar take Jamerica in the house. Me and Dub will hold them off!" Boo Boo yelled.

"No, put your guns down. We outnumbered," Damar said. He was hoping that those renegades would take them and spare Jamerica and the baby.

Dub and Boo Boo dropped their guns and held their hands up. "Man, if we make it through this, I'ma kill Fresh on sight," Dub promised.

The buggies stopped right in front of them, their attackers jumped out armed and walked over. A short dark skinned Jamaican stepped forward. For some odd reason he looked familiar to Damar. His troops lined up behind him.

Damar stepped in front of Jamerica. "We surrender, please spare my girl and my baby." He held his head high.

The Jamaican wiped his pink lips with the back of his hand and looked Damar up and down, then he got a folded piece of paper out of his pocket and looked over it. A smirk came over his face, then he showed the paper to the other man standing to his right. He nodded. "Ahoa, Ben's bruda." The one holding the paper smiled and looked at Damar, then he bowed his head at him.

Damar's brow wrinkled. He didn't know what this was all about. Dub and Boo Boo looked at each other just as confused as Damar. The Jamaican then turned to his people. "Listen everyone, this is the man who helps us provide for our families. The King."

Then he stepped to Damar and extended his hand. "I'm Jacob, Ben's bruda. He sends me twenty thousand dollars a month, thanks to you," Jacob said.

"Ben?" Damar questioned upon accepting his hand shake.

The Jamaican chuckled realizing Damar didn't know his brother by that name. "Taz, is mi bruda," he said with a smile of pride.

At that moment, Damar knew why the man looked familiar and exhaled a sigh of relief. *Damn, I gotta have nine lives,* Damar thought to himself.

"Ya mon, mi bruda called me and said you may need some help. Gava is a bad man. He use his power for evil," Jacob said, looking at Gava's mansion.

"Not anymore, his money don't mean shit in hell," Damar said, confirming Gava's death.

"You sure he's dead?" Jacob asked as he did a quick glance at the mansion.

Damar nodded, "Just as sure as a fat kid loves cake."

"Ah Iree, mon, now we gotta get you off the island." As they started walking toward the buggies, Jacob stopped. He heard something. He cupped his ear. "You here that?"

"Yeah, it sounds like it's coming this way," Damar said just as a fleet of trucks came into view north of the mansion.

"Your people?" Damar asked on alert.

"Nah!" Jacob shook his head with a disturbing look on his face. Then he turned to his men, "Bloodfire, hold them off, we'll be waiting at the ferry."

He then turned to Damar. "They're Gava's men, hurry we must go."

Damar quickly helped Jamerica into the buggy before hopping in himself. Dub and Boo Boo jumped in another buggy. Jacob climbed in and hit the gas pedal. The tires spun in the grass and the dune buggy jetted away. Jacob grabbed his radio and hit the side button. "We ran into trouble, lower de ramp. I repeat lower de ramp."

Damar wrapped his arms around Jamerica to deflect the dust, since there was nothing he could do about the bumpy ride.

Once out of harm's way Damar, looked back toward the mansion, it was dark, but he saw sparks flying and the other buggy trailing behind.

Jacob drove a mile down from Gava's dock to a secluded area. Shielded by tall Evergreens was a thirty foot ferry. The ramp was lowered just as Jacob requested, the two buggies sped over the ramp and parked in the lower deck.

Damar carefully walked Jamerica to a customized couch on the ferry. She quickly pulled the blanket away from Prince's face. He was crying so she rocked and placed kisses on his forehead until he stopped. Then she looked at Damar who was glued to her side. "I love you, Damar." She then sighed. "Baby, while I was on the island, Gava he—"

"Shhhhh!" Damar hushed her and cradled her head against his chest. "It's over now, baby," he said while the ocean breeze cooled his sweaty face.

A few minutes later, Dub and Boo Boo walked up behind him.

"I can't believe Fresh left us for dead," Boo Boo said, slamming his fist in his palm.

Damar's jaw muscles flexed and he cut his eyes up at Boo Boo. "And he gonna pay for it."

"Yeah, he's a dead man walking," Dub added.

Suddenly it hit Damar, the ferry wasn't moving. "Yo, Boo Boo, see why we still here."

"Alright!" Boo Boo walked over to Jacob.

Damar looked at Jamerica, "I ain't leaving your side until we get out of Jamaica."

When Boo Boo approached Jacob he was standing by the rail looking for any signs of his men.

"Yo, Jacob, why we ain't moving yet?"

Jacob kept his eyes sunk into the darkness and replied, "I'm waiting on my men. I won't leave them on the island."

"Oh, okay, I'll tell my boss." Boo Boo walked back over to Damar.

"What he say?"

"He said he's waiting on his peeps."

Dub-Sac reached for his Glock. "Fuck that, we need to go."

"Chill, Dub, it's all about loyalty. If I was in his shoes, I would wait on my niggas, too," Damar said.

Dub sighed and thought for a minute. Damar was right. "A'ight, I'ma chill."

At that moment, they heard a gunshot. It echoed throughout the boat. Damar covered Jamerica and yelled to Dub and Boo Boo, "Go see what's going on!"

They both rushed to the front of the boat.

"Mi people!" Jacob said, sounding relieved.

"Let me see," Dub said as he put on his night goggles. He saw four trucks heading in their direction. Off impulse, he grabbed his M-16. "Nah them Gava's people." And began firing at them.

Boo Boo put his goggles on and started shooting, too.

Jacob ran toward the wheel and whistled to the captain. When he got his attention, he shouted. "Go, go, go!"

The captain quickly pushed the throttle forward and the ferry slowly pulled away from the shore.

When the trucks finally reached the shoreline. The ferry was 200 feet away. Gava's men jumped out of their vehicles and started shooting at the ferry until it was out of gun range.

Once Damar only heard the clashing waves and the ferry's engine, he let go of Jamerica and they looked at each other.

Jamerica thought she saw fear in his eyes and rubbed the side of his face. "We're gonna be alright, baby. God got us."

Damar leaned up and kissed her long and hard. When they stopped to breathe, he shook his head. "Baby, I thought I would never see you again."

Jamerica smiled and placed her hand on his. "I know, my king. I thought I was going to die without you. So I could only imagine how you felt. But guess what?"

"What baby?" Damar said, trying to hold back his tears. But he couldn't and they came streaming down his face.

Jamerica wiped his cheek and said softly, God gave me enough strength for the both of us."

Boo Boo and Dub walked up on their blind side.

"We made it, bruh." Boo Boo said, breathing heavy.

Damar looked up at Boo Boo. "Not yet, big homie. We still in Jamaica."

Jacob walked up shortly after and said, "Hey, mi bruda, you're safe for now."

Damar then turned to Jacob and asked, "Can this ferry go any faster? I'm sure they have a boat too."

Jacob smiled. "Don't worry. I took care of that."

***

Back on the island…

Gava's men drove back to the dock hoping to catch up to the ferry with their speed boats.

Unfortunately, the two motor boats occupying the dock were engulfed in flames because Jacob and his people had set them on fire when they arrived on the island.

Gava's men stood on the dock watching their boats burn. One of the men pulled out his phone and called his superior. Who answered on the second ring.

"Gwan?"

"Hey, boss, they got away. Gava's dead and they got the American girl but we have four hostages," the man said.

"Aha, good. Bring them to the camp."

Chapter 12
7 a.m. Montego Bay

There were two black BMWs parked on the pier waiting on the ferry. When Jacob saw the cars, he called one of the drivers to make sure everything was good before he let the passengers off of the boat. Once the driver confirmed all was good, Jacob told Damar they had to leave the big guns on the ferry but they could bring their hand guns. Then three of his men boarded the boat to escort Damar and his crew safely to the cars.

Damar held on to Jamerica as they walked across the dock, above the turquoise sea. The sun was bright orange and the breeze was brisk. Damar took account of this tropical place at the same time keeping a hawk eye on everything moving. When they reached the car, a bulky Jamaican opened the back door to let Damar and Jamerica in, then Jacob hopped in the passenger seat. Boo Boo and Dub climbed in the other BMW and the caravan pulled away from the busy port.

A mile up the road, Damar interrupted Jacob's conversation with the driver. "Excuse me, Jacob."

Jacob turned and looked between the seats. "What's upa, mi bruda?"

"I hope we're heading to the airport." Damar said.

"Not yet. We have tree international airports here, and I'm pretty sure Gava's people have reported us to the authorities. So they would be waiting for us to show up at anyone of them. Let's wait until this afternoon, I think it will safer by then."

"So how you plan on getting us the fuck out of Jamaica?"

"I have a friend in Negril, he has a private jet. I'll call him and get him to take you." But until I speak with him, I'm taking you to my sister's place in Bogue Village."

"What if he can't take us?" Damar said.

"Mi bruda, if the price is right, he'll take you to the moon and back."

"Cool, call 'em and let me know the price." Damar said.

Jacob nodded and turned back around in his seat. "No problem, mon." He made the call.

Damar turned to look at Jamerica while baby Prince was asleep in her arms. "You okay, baby?" he asked with gentle concern.

Jamerica shook her head. "Not really. I'm sore and I'm bleeding through my clothes."

Damar rubbed her hand, then he leaned up and said to Jacob, "Hey, my girl just had a baby. She needs a nurse ASAP."

Jacob nodded *okay* while he was on the phone talking with his friend. After his conversation, he turned to Damar, "Mi friend said he'll do it for five thousand."

"Cool, I got it. But yo, we need passports," Damar said.

"That's no problem, mi bruda. When we get to mi sister's house, I will need to take your pictures. Mi bruda in-law makes fake ID's and passports."

"A'ight, run that shit. How long before our flight?"

"Mi friend, Michael, said he'll be there at 2 o'clock," Jacob replied over his shoulder.

Damar looked at his watch, it was 7:30 a.m. "Fuck that's another six hours."

"Don't worry you'll be safe where I'm taking you." Jacob assured him and turned his attention to the busy streets.

Damar checked his rear. The other BMW was still following close behind. Both cars had dark tint. Damar couldn't see anything but the driver's knuckles on the steering wheel. So he took out his phone to make sure his boys was good.

He dialed up Boo Boo. He answered on the first ring.

"What's up, bruh?"

"Ya'll straight?"

"Yeah, I'm just hungry as a muthafucka!" Boo Boo said, chuckling.

"Ha, ha, for once I'm with you on that. Yo, Jacob taking us to his sister's house. He got us a plane, but it ain't gonna be here until two. So it's gonna be a minute. Just remember we're not out of danger yet. So when we get to the house, y'all don't get too comfortable. We got to stay on point at all times, you feel me?"

"I gotcha, bruh."

"How's your gun wounds?" Damar asked.

"Just a little sore, but I got the bleeding to stop." Both bullets went through, so I'm straight," Boo Boo said.

"Alright, Jacob got a nurse coming over to take a look at Jamerica, I'll get her to stitch you up while she's there."

"That's what's up. How's her and the baby doing?" Boo Boo asked.

They look a'ight, won't really know until the nurse takes a look at them." Ah, what Dub doin?"

Boo Boo glanced at Dub and smiled. "Shit, he sitting here looking crazy as usual."

"Ha, ha, that's what's up. 'Cause if he starts looking anything but crazy, something wrong with his ass," Damar said.

Boo Boo laughed again. "I know, right."

"Well, I'll see you when we get to the house."

"Bet." Boo Boo ended the call.

***

Ten minutes later…

The BMWs were pulling into a narrow drive way that led up to a small brick house surrounded by a white cinder block wall. Two palm trees shared the front lawn and an old Honda was taking up space on the side of the house. When they parked, the driver got out and opened the door for Jamerica.

Damar got out behind her and held the small of her back. The back of her dress was spotted with blood. By the look on her face, Damar could tell she was in pain.

So he took baby Prince out of her hands, "I got him. Yo, Boo Boo, carry Jamerica in the house."

Boo Boo walked over and scooped her into his arms.

Jacob told his driver to come back at 1:30 to take them to the airport and he escorted Damar and his crew inside.

Damar observed his surroundings as they walked up the driveway. The neighborhood looked peaceful, the air was cool and soothing but smelled like burning trash. Damar saw a neighbor peeping out of her window. She ducked away when they made eye contact. Then Damar heard a chain snatch followed by a dog barking from behind the house.

When they walked in the house a thick-set light-skinned woman approached them skeptically. She had on a red summer dress. "Jacob, who dat you bring to mi house?"

"Lisa, this is Ben's boss. They're gonna stay here for a couple of hours."

"Nice to meet you," she said in her thick Jamaican accent.

Damar did a head nod. "Nice to meet you, too."

"Hmmm, what's wrong with the gyal?" She pointed at Jamerica.

"She just had a baby, can you see about her?" Jacob asked.

Damar whipped his head at Jacob, "Hey! I told you she needed a nurse. Your sister don't look like no nurse to me."

"Hee, hee, hee, she look more like a prosti—"

"Dub!" Damar stopped him before he called Lisa a hoe.

Lisa held her tongue but gave Dub a salty look.

"Be easy, mi bruda, Lisa is a registered nurse." Then Jacob cut his eye at Dub and added, "And she also kick-boxes."

Dub eyeballed her and huffed. *Yeah bitch put them big ass feet on me, I'ma shoot the shit outta her.*

Damar then handed Dub baby Prince, "Hold him." Then he went in his pocket and pulled out a bankroll and generously gave Lisa two hundred dollars. "Here, is this enough?"

Lisa kindly accepted Damar's offer, "Thank you." She tucked the money into her bra.

"Oh and my big homie might need some stitches, he got shot in the arm."

Lisa's eyes bucked. "Shot?"

Damar didn't want to go into details, so he peeled off an additional hundred dollars and handed it to her.

This time Lisa didn't reach for it, she just crossed her arms.

Damar was getting impatient. "Look, ma'am, no disrespect but I ain't got time for twenty-one questions. If you don't want to help us, please call someone who can."

"Lisa these are good people," Jacob said.

Lisa looked at Boo Boo then her eyes rolled over to Dub-Sac. "If they're so good, why did someone shoot him?"

Boo Boo walked over with Jamerica in his arms and said calmly, "Hey, Miss Lady, you don't have to worry about me just see about her."

Boo Boo's unselfish comment softened Lisa up. She looked at Jamerica, she was so pretty. Her beauty made Lisa smile, "Take them to my room."

Jacob stopped them. "Wait one second. Let me snap your pictures so I can email them to mi bruda in-law. It will only take a couple of hours for him to make the credentials you need and I'll go get them when he's done."

"A'ight," Damar said. Jacob snapped his pic first.

Then Boo Boo put Jamerica down so she could get her pic taken. Boo Boo and Dub were last to get their pictures snapped.

After the awkward photo shoot, Boo Boo picked Jamerica back up. Damar leaned over and kissed her on the forehead. "Muah! You're gonna be alright, baby." Then he turned and took baby Prince out of Dub's hands and he and Boo Boo followed Lisa to the bedroom.

Dub shook his head as they disappeared to the back. "Feisty."

Jacob nodded, "Yeah, that's mi sister."

Damar and Boo Boo returned from the back in no time. Boo Boo stepped to Jacob, rubbing his stomach. "Man, what y'all got to eat?"

Damar cracked a smile, "You got that shit right, sounds like a dog in my stomach."

Jacob chuckled. "Come, I'll find ya someting."

They followed Jacob to the kitchen, and he fixed them each a plate of rice & peas, curry goat, fried fish with spicy vinegar and scotch bonnet peppers, roasted corn and mango juice.

When they sat down, Dub and Boo Boo started digging in until Damar stopped them. "Hey, hey, hey, hey, bless your food first. We made it through hell today, God spared us again."

Dub and Boo Boo looked at each other before bowing their head. Damar then lead the prayer.

"God, we like to thank you for watching over us today and giving me my babies back. And thank you for your grace and mercy. May you bless this food we are about to receive. In your name we pray."

"Amen!" they said together. After Damar blessed the food, they all dug in.

Chapter 13
Three Hours Ago

Fresh sat behind the cockpit on an empty gas can with his Glock aimed at the back of Dennis' head. He didn't feel bad for leaving his crew, he actually felt good, and a big weight had been lifted off his shoulders. Now he had no one to answer to, no one to envy. He was the King now. He smiled at himself but only for a mere moment. He had to figure out a way to get rid of the pilot.

First, he cleared his mind so he could think. He looked around the chopper, then it hit him when he saw a parachute on the shelf. He rushed over and grabbed it and sat back down on the can. He leaned forward, "Hey, Dennis."

"Yeah what is it?" Dennis replied with an attitude.

So Fresh pressed the Glock harder against his head. "Man, you in a fucked up situation right now, so I advise you to take some of that bass out your voice. Now what's our twenty?"

Dennis looked at his panel, "We'll be flying over Tampa in ten/twelve minutes." Dennis yelled over his shoulder.

Fresh lowered his gun and slipped the parachute on his back, then he took out his phone and made a call. When the person answered, Fresh didn't give them time to say anything. He spoke briefly, "Can't talk just pick me up at the bus station in Tampa."

Click!

After he hung up, he pulled his sleeves up and looked at his watch. He waited nine minutes and then he yelled to Dennis. "We over Tampa yet?"

Dennis glanced back at his panel to check. "Be there in two minutes."

Fresh then put a helmet and goggles on. He looked at his watch and counted down the seconds. When his watch reached exactly two minutes he went and pushed the button to open the side door. The cool Florida wind blew in, causing a slight turbulence. Before Dennis could turn his head to see what Fresh was doing, his brains and teeth splattered across the windshield. Fresh then tucked his Glock and jumped out the helicopter.

***

Back on Navy Island 10 a.m.
Camp site

The four hostages that Gava's men captured were sitting on their knees in a single filed line, with their hands tied behind their back. The green uniforms they wore were now dark green from the sweat pouring from their overheated bodies. They had been sitting in the sun since it came up hours ago. Ten armed men were standing behind them while a distinguished Jamaican, by the name of Isaac, paced in front of them in army fatigues.

"I hold you all responsible for Gava's death and you will be executed. Unless…" he paused with his finger in the air. "…you tell me who you work for and where can I find him. Then I will just cut off one of your hands."

The hostages looked straight ahead as if Isaac wasn't speaking to them. He waited another minute to see if anyone was going to volunteer some information, still they remained silent. So he stepped to the side and nodded to the armed men. Then he held up his arm. The armed Jamaicans raised their rifles, when Isaac dropped his hand they filled the hostage to the far right full of holes. Blood splattered on the face of the man sitting next to him before the riddled body fell to the side.

Isaac then stepped back in front of the hostages. "Now, do you know who you work for?" He looked into the teary eyes of the three remaining men.

They were frightened, yet no one said a word or looked him in the eyes. As he slowly walked around them with his hands cupped in the front of him, he had patience like a chess player so he gave them a few more minutes to decide their fate. He walked back to the front of them. "I admire your loyalty, but there comes a time in life when you have to swallow your pride in order to see another day." He finally said and took his knife from its casing. He then grabbed one of the hostages by his dreads and put the knife to his Adams apple. The man still did not break, he just closed his eyes and a tear rolled down his cheek. Isaac pulled the man's head back. "This is what happens when you hold your pride to close to your heart." He slit the prisoner's throat and pushed him on his face.

The man's blood quickly soaked up the soil under him. The hostage next to him made the grave mistake of looking down at his deceased comrade. At that moment he didn't want to die, his wife and children flashed before him. He was scared. It was obvious that his captors had no mercy. His heart galloped at the speed of light, as Isaac stepped over to him. His mouth trembled when he saw the blood dripping from the concave blade. The young soldier knew that death was imminent if he didn't give them what they wanted.

"Two down, two to go." Isaac brought the knife down to the young man's throat.

As soon as the ridge of the knife touched his skin, he shouted. "Wait! I'll tell you everyting."

The prisoner beside him turned and said angrily, "Shut up, you fool. Shut up!" Then he rammed his head into the blabber's side and fell on top of him.

One of the soldiers quickly separated them and shot the rebellious one in the head.

Boc! Boc!

His head jerked and then he fell on his back.

The last hostage was snatched to his feet and held by the crook of his arm. His lips were parched from dehydration and he could barely stand on his own.

"Wata, please." He begged as his head bobbled.

Isaac held up his pointer finger, "First, tell me who you work for," He wiped the blade clean on his pants.

The prisoner swallowed the last drop of saliva in his mouth and took a deep breath and confessed. "Jacob Mandela."

Isaac placed his knife back in the case, then asked, "Where does he live?"

The prisoner moaned. "Montego Bay on Coconut Street."

"What's the tenement number?" Isaac asked.

"1427." The prisoner said before his legs gave and he slipped from the soldiers hand and hit the ground.

Isaac was almost satisfied. He pointed to a soldier on his right flank and said, "You can give him some wata now."

The soldier took his canteen off of his shoulder and started pouring the water over on the prisoner's face. When the cool water splashed the man's face his mouth went agape. The soldier teased him by pouring it everywhere but in his mouth. The poor man sucked up more air than water.

Isaac threw his head back and laughed. His soldiers joined in on the laugher. When the canteen was empty, the soldier dropped it on the ground. The prisoner rolled on his side and sadly watched a single drop of water fall from the canteen.

All of a sudden Isaac stopped laughing. He frowned and walked up and stood over the captive who was repeating to himself, "Please free me. Please free me. Please." He was weak and delirious.

Isaac reached behind his back and gripped his beretta, "You should have died a man and not a coward." He whipped his gun out and fired two shots into the man's chest.

Boc! Boc!

His body fell, stretched out and jerked a couple of times. Then he died with his eyes open.

Then Isaac turned to his general, Marcus Randolph, who was just as heartless as he was. He also enjoyed seeing people suffer before they died. "General Randolph I want Jacob right here by sunset," Isaac said, pointing at the bloody ground.

The general clapped his heels together. "Yes, sir." He saluted Isaac and did an about-face and walked away.

Chapter 14
Back at Jacob sister's house

After tending to Jamerica and baby Prince, Lisa went in the laundry room and started washing clothes. Damar was in the bedroom with Jamerica asleep in the recliner. Big Boo Boo was in the front yard on his phone talking to Sandy. Dub-Sac was in the living room trying to get Lisa's green and yellow parrot to say his name, but all the bird kept saying was Bob Marley.

"Look, you dumbass bird. Read my lips. Dub-Sac, Dub-Sac."

The parrot walked side to side and blurted out, *Bob Marley, Bob Marley.*

Dub-Sac shook his head. "No, no, no, bird. You just as crazy as me. You sure you ain't no cuckoo bird dressed in a parrot suit? Now let's try this shit again, say, Duuub-Sac, Duub-Sac." The parrot started whistling the Sanford and Son theme song.

When he got tired of whistling, he asked Dub-Sac for a cracker. *Brroc, Charlie want a cracker.*

"Oooh, that's your name? Charlie's dumbass wanna cracker, huh?"

Brroc. Charlie wanna a cracker.

Dub-Sac looked around and made sure nobody was in the vicinity. The coast was clear so he ran to the kitchen and went through the cabinets and found a box of saltines. He opened the box and took out a sleeve and took out a cracker. He licked both sides of it, then he went in his pocket and pulled out a small bag of cocaine. He opened the bag and sprinkled some on each side of the cracker. He left the box on the table and went back into the living room.

Charlie was still ranting about a cracker. “Damn, chill, Charlie, you ‘bout as greedy as Boo Boo. Here you go.” He broke the bird off a corner. Charlie quickly devoured it.

“Hee, hee, hee, hee, your ass getting high today.”

When Charlie finished the whole cracker, Dub rubbed his hands together. “Now it’s time for me to get high.” He pulled out the bag of coke. It was under a gram, so he decided to do it in just two hits. He pulled a single bill out of his pocket and rolled it up like a straw. Then he poured the coke in the palm of his hand and stuck the end of the bill up his nose. Right when he was about to sniff, somebody came busting through the front door.

Boom!

Dub jumped and dropped everything and reached for his Glock and then turned around.

“Hey, it’s just me,” Jacob said, throwing his hands up. In one hand was a zip lock bag of something and a black brief-case in the other hand.

“Damn, my nigga, you almost got your ass shot,” Dub said.

“Mi bad. Sometime the door get stuck and you have to kick it.” Jacob said while walking into the kitchen.

Dub-Sac watched him until he was out of sight. “Well, y’all niggas need to get that shit fixed,” he mumbled. “Made me drop my shit all on the floor.” He kneeled down and scooped what he could off of the floor. When he stood he saw the coke had too much trash in it, so he dumped it into Char-lie’s food bowl.

Then a bad smell grazed his nose. He looked toward the kitchen. “I hope that’s weed and not that niggas armpits,” Dub said to himself and went to go check it out.

When he entered the kitchen, Jacob was rolling a blunt at the island bar. Dub hopped on the bar stool and propped his elbows up on the mesquite counter top. “Whatcha got, my nigga?”

“Good Jamaican bud. Guaranteed to put your wood in the dirt.” Jacob bragged while licking the blunt.

Dub raised a brow, “Is that right?”

“Iree mon, smell it.”

Dub took the bag of weed and smelled it. “Dis shit stank! That’s what I smelt, I thought it was you smelling like a baby Billy goat.”

“Ha, ha, ha,” Jacob laughed and put the blunt to his mouth and lit it with a Bic lighter. He puffed and blew out a big cloud of smoke.

Dub sat up right on the barstool, “Weed really ain’t my thang, but let me see what you working with.”

Jacob passed the blunt and Dub hit it twice. He exhaled. “Why you roll it so small? Where I’m from we roll blunts big as your thumb.”

“Aha, it’s just that good, mi bruda.”

Dub smacked his lips together. “It got a good taste to it. But what that coke hitting like around here?”

“Very, very good, a gram will last you all dey.”

“No shit,” Dub said while passing the blunt back to Jacob.

“Yeah, I once did two grams and I fucked for tree deys.”

“Shiit I don’t wanna stay in no pussy that long. Nigga fuck around and have a heart attack or seizure or something,” Dub said. They both burst out laughing.

Suddenly they heard a loud scream. They got up from the table and rushed in to the living room. The distressful cry was coming from Lisa. She was having a fit in front of Charlie’s cage pulling on her hair and screaming. “Oh, no! Not my baby!”

Jacob ran over to his sister and saw Charlie laying on his back with his legs sticking straight up. He pulled her close and started rubbing her back. "Don't cry, it's gonna be okay."

Damar ran from the bedroom with his Glock in hand and stood beside Dub-Sac. Once he saw that there was no need for his gun, he concealed it. "What's wrong with her?"

Dub shrugged his shoulders, "Shiiit I think her bird died."

Lisa was crying uncontrollably so Jacob took her into the bedroom. When he returned, he got Charlie out the cage and placed him in a shoe box.

Damar and Dub came up behind him. "She gonna be alright?" Damar asked.

"In time she will be." Jacob replied.

"Ole bird musta been really special," Damar said, looking in the shoebox.

Jacob sighed and looked toward Lisa's bedroom. "Twelve years ago Lisa found out she couldn't have children. She really took it hard. I found Charlie at the animal rescue center and gave him to her for a birthday present. He became her baby, so you see he was more than a talking bird, he was family," Jacob said.

"Damn, sorry to hear that," Damar said.

Jacob held up his hands up. "I don't know why he kill over. Lisa took him to the vet once a month for a checkup. They said he was healthy." Then he turned and went out back to bury the bird.

Damar looked at Dub. He had a guilty look on his face. "Why you looking all suspect. What did you do?"

Dub quickly responded "Nah, my nigga, I ain't did shit." Then he went and sat on the couch to watch TV.

Damar shook his head and went back in the room with Jamerica and the baby.

Chapter 15

Coconut Street Noon time

Iris Mandela was in the kitchen washing dishes while looking out of her window. The breeze coming from outside was nice and the atmosphere was peaceful today. The street was filled with happy children.

Suddenly, her state of serenity came to an abrupt end when a fleet of camouflage jeeps bombarded the street. They pulled up in front of her building. Armed men evacuated their vehicles like there were on a serious mission.

Iris watched with suspicion as they approached her building. Moments later, she heard her front door come crashing in. Her first reaction was to grab her three year old twins and get them to safety. She ran out the kitchen through the living room, passed her intruders and went to her children's room. The soldiers ran after her.

When she got there, they were on the bed watching TV. She quickly snatched them up by their arms and hid them in the closet. She told them to be quiet and don't come out until she came back. Then she ran out of the room and ran smack into one of the men in the doorway. He grabbed her by the hair and drug her back into the bedroom and shoved her on the floor. An infantry of soldiers swarmed around her.

Iris was shaking like a leaf on a tree as she stood up. Her lips quivered. "What do you want?"

The soldiers stepped to the side and made a path for General Randolph. He came forward and got straight to the point. "Where's Jacob Mandela?" His voice was thick and scary.

"I-I-I don't know. He left me months ago." She cried.

The general smiled because he was told something different. He glanced around the multicolored room. He saw cartoons playing on the TV and toys scattered on the floor and a red crayon was at his feet. He reached down and picked it up and held it to his face. "I wonder who this belongs to." He gave his men a hand signal to search the room.

Iris's eyes followed the soldiers around the room. One looked under the beds, one looked behind the dresser. When she saw one reaching for the closet door, she threw herself at the mercy of the general.

"Please! Please don't hurt my children. She begged as tears rolled down her face. I'll tell you where he is."

Her children were more important. Also, she knew she could call Jacob when they left.

After Iris told the general where Jacob was, he ordered one of his soldiers to strangle her. The soldier grabbed her by the neck with both hands and pulled her up from the floor. He laced his fingers and began choking her. Her eyes bulged out and a large vein appeared on her forehead. Iris clawed his hands with her fingernails, while her legs treaded underneath her. Her struggling made the man squeeze even harder. Her coco brown skin turned reddish brown as her oxygen was violently being cut off. She kicked a few more times before her legs and arms went limp. The soldier then released her and she dropped to the floor.

The general then walked over to the closet and snatch the door open. The twins flitched and huddled up in the closet. Their eyes was big and shiny. When the general saw that they weren't old enough to say anything, he closed the closet door and turned to his soldiers. "Let's go!" Then led his men out the door.

As they were leaving, the general saw a family photo with Iris, the twins and more than likely Jacob on the coffee table. He took the picture out of the frame and slipped it in his pocket and left.

***

Back at Bogue Village…

While Damar was looking out the living room window, Boo Boo was on the recliner talking to Sandy on the phone and Dub-Sac was on the love seat bobbing his head to the smooth reggae music coming from Lisa's entertainment system. Lisa and Jamerica was on the couch talking. Jamerica felt better after she took a bath and put on some clean clothes that Lisa gave her.

Jacob was pacing the living room because his wife, Iris, wasn't answering her phone, which was very rare. He walked over to Damar, cussing under his breathe.

"You alright?" Damar asked still looking out the window.

"Mi wife not answering her phone."

"Maybe she's busy, my nigga."

"Busy or no busy, she always answer de phone."

Damar didn't give him a second reply, right then he didn't give a rat's ass about Jacob's problems. His concern was getting the fuck out of Jamaica. He'd stayed long enough, he was running out of patience. All of a sudden it began to thunder and then came the rain crashing down on the tin roof. The noise was annoying so Dub got up and walked to the window. He saw the sun was still shining but it was raining hard.

"You know, Jacob, some Americans believe that the devil is beating his wife when it's raining and the suns out," Damar said.

"Shiit, look like he whooping dat ass good, too." Dub replied just when the BMWs turned on the street.

Damar saw them first, he glanced at his watch, *1:20 perfect timing* he thought. "Yo, it's time to ride." He rushed over to get Jamerica and baby Prince.

Boo Boo stood and ended his call with Sandy and walked to help Damar. "What you want me to do?" He asked, towering over Damar and Jamerica.

"You and Dub just cover us," Damar said, helping Jamerica off of the couch.

Lisa stood and gave Jamerica a friendly hug. "Come see me the next time you're in Jamaica."

Jamerica smiled. "I will and thank you for helping us."

Then Dub and Boo Boo escorted them to the car. Before they got in, Boo Boo checked both cars inside and out.

Once in the comfort of the Beamer, Jacob yelled to Damar from the front seat. "De rain wata come just in time, aha?"

Damar glanced out the window at the rain. "Yeah, I guess it did. How far is the airport?"

"Sangster is five miles from here." Jacob replied.

"Cool." Damar looked back at his crew in the other car behind him.

When they got to the end of the road they made a left on Maple Street. They didn't see the fleet of jeeps coming up the road to the right, heading toward Lisa's house. Had Damar's car came to the junction a minute early they would have crossed paths.

By the time the BMWs entered the city limits the rain was at a drizzle. The street venders were resetting their stands, so they could continue their daily hustle.

***

Lisa had just locked her door when she heard sliding tires outside. She peeked out of the window and saw four jeeps parked in front of her house. She didn't panic until the armed soldiers jumped out and ran toward her. Before she could open the door it came crashing down. General Randolph barged in with his soldiers following behind him.

Lisa stepped back and got into a fighting stance. "What the Bumboclot you want!"

General Randolph stepped closer to her and asked with authority, "Where's Jacob?"

Lisa frowned. "Whose gonna pay for mi door."

General Randolph looked at his soldiers and laughed. Then he asked again, "Where's Jacob?"

Lisa snapped. "He don't live here!"

The general quickly raised his hand for his soldiers to search the place. Before the first soldier could get past the living room. Lisa jumped in front of him. He pushed her to the floor. She jumped up and punched him in the face. Another soldier grabbed her from behind and twisted her arm up. She tugged ferociously but couldn't break his grasp. So she stumped his foot. He yelled and released her. Lisa turned around and kicked him in the stomach. He staggered and fell on her coffee table. Then another soldier reached for her and she blocked his attempt and kicked him in the nuts. When he bent over, she round kicked him in the chin and he flew back and landed on her glass table. A third soldier came up behind her and clubbed her with his baton. Lisa dropped instantly to the floor. She wasn't out cold but she was out of commission. She moaned in agony as blood poured from the back of her head.

The general stood over her, "I admire your courage."

Lisa slowly crawled on all fours and looked up at him. "Fuck you!" She spit on his boots.

One of the soldiers bent down and wiped his boot. At the same time another soldier was coming from the kitchen with a phone in his hand. He walked over and handed it to the general. "Read the text, sir."

The general held the phone up and read the text.

Message: Yo Jacob, I'm at Sangster. Where are you? Received Sat Oct 29 1:44pm.

After reading the text, the general put the phone in his pocket and looked at his watch. It was 1:45p.m. He had no time to waste. He quickly blew his whistle and his men stopped searching the house and came together in the living room. Then he walked over to Lisa and snatched his gun out and aimed it at her head.

She looked at him with eyes full of rage. "I'm not afraid to die!"

General Randolph chuckled. "Good." He pulled the trigger.

Boc!

The back of Lisa's head exploded and she collapsed, then the general placed his revolver back in his holster and waved to his men. "Let's go, he's headed to Sangster."

***

Sangster International Airport 2:01

When the BMWs parked beside an RV, Jacob went in his pocket in search of his cellphone. He didn't feel it. He checked his other pocket and between the seats. Nothing. His phone was nowhere to be found. He sucked his teeth. "Bumboclot! I must have left it at Lisa's. Let me see your phone." He asked the driver.

The driver reached down and got his phone from the door panel and handed it to him. Jacob took the phone and dialed a number. It rung once.

"Gwan?"

"We're here," Jacob said.

"I'm on runway 6."

"Good." Jacob hung up. He opened the brief case he had sitting on his lap. He took out the fake ID's and passports and handed them to Damar before they all got out of the car. Dub and Boo Boo jumped out their car and rushed over to Damar's side.

Damar touched the small of Jamerica's back as he was helping her out the car. "Yo, y'all keep your fingers crossed we ain't out of this shit yet."

"We gotcha, bruh," Boo Boo said and then they all followed Jacob in to the airport.

When they got inside, Jacob told Damar where the plane was located and gave him a description of his friend Michael. Next, he gave him a warm farewell. "I guess this is where we say goodbye." Jacob extended his hand out to Damar.

Damar gave him a firm hand shake, "Yeah, this is it. Thank you, Jacob, for your hospitality. When I get back to the states and get situated, I would like you to come visit. All expenses paid, just bring ya ass."

Jacob chuckled, "Okay, mi bruda." Then he faced Jamerica and took a bow. "It was a pleasure meeting you, ma'am."

Jamerica smiled. "Thank you so much, Jacob. And when you come bring Lisa with you."

Jacob returned the smile. "I sure will." Then he shook Dub and Boo Boo's hands and the four headed toward customs.

Once they made it through safely, Damar squeezed Jamerica and kissed the top of her head. "We're almost there, baby. You alright?"

She looked up at him. "Yeah, I love you."

"I love you, too." Then he looked back at Jacob and threw up the peace sign. While Jacob and his driver were waving back, Damar saw several policemen and soldiers heading toward them with their weapons out.

Damar stopped and started pointing behind them. By the time Jacob realized what was going on, it was too late. The policemen were on them, ordering them to get on the ground.

"Fuck!" Damar turned around and kept walking. There was nothing he could do.

Chapter 16
A Couple of Hours Later

There was a worldwide news flash. A Russian helicopter crashed in Tampa, Florida killing five by standers and injuring twenty-one people. Damar was listening about the crash over the radio during his flight back to Ricardo's landing strip in Phoenix, Arizona. It had to be Ricardo's chopper.

The news reporter said they believe the aircraft belonged to the Russians and the government wasn't sure what their motive was here in the United States. But the deadly crash was under investigation.

The bad news didn't sit too well with Damar. Not because Dennis or Fresh died in the crash but because he didn't have a part in Fresh's death. But the good part about this whole ordeal was that Jamerica and baby Prince were alive and well.

After Damar spoke with Ricardo, he checked into a hotel in Los Angeles California and he hired a private nurse to attend to Jamerica and Prince. Then he contacted Taz and told him to fly out to Cali so he could personally thank him. He sent Dub-Sac and Boo Boo to the stash house in Fort Meyers to get the millions he had stashed in the walls.

Damar and Jamerica were so happy to be reunited again. It was such a joyous moment. Earlier she wanted to tell Damar what Gava done to her, but now she just wanted to forget and think about their future together, the wedding and raising baby Prince.

Damar felt the same way, lying next to Jamerica holding their baby, it felt like they were meant to be. The feeling inside of him made him realize she really had his heart.

By sunrise, Jamerica had drifted off to sleep but baby Prince was wide awake laying between them. His bright eyes were trying to focus on Damar leaning over him.

"What's up, lil' man. Coochie, coochie, coo," Damar said, tickling Prince's cheek.

Baby Prince smiled just a little. He had the same crooked smile that Damar had. Damar's eyes teared up. He never thought he'd see this day. He didn't think he deserved God's mercy, especially after all the drugs he sold in his lifetime. He had a part in destroying millions of lives and he'd killed lots of people. But time after time, the man upstairs proved that there was hope for every man.

Now looking down at his baby boy made him see the light. His son brought a new meaning to his life. He wanted to be around and watch this little baby grow up to be a man. For the first time ever, he wanted to grow old and say the hell with the fast life. This life of crime that only promise death or life behind bars.

The devil had took him through hell with gasoline drawers on time and time again, but he never broke or folded. Each time Damar conquered something he felt more invincible than before and the truth was when he walked through the valley of the shadow of death and feared no evil. It was God's rod and staff that comforted him. Now it was time to make a change for the better. He wasn't going to let being a wanted man cripple his true destiny because his life was far from over. It had just begun. But first he had to be a man and tell Sunja that shit was over between them.

Chapter 17
Fort Myers, Florida

Dub-Sac and Big Boo Boo spent hours ripping out walls in the stash house. The money was gone. "Damar ain't gonna like this!" Boo Boo said, shaking his head.

"Man, a muthafucka had to be watching us. Nobody knew we stashed the loot here, but me, you and Fresh. And we know he didn't take it, 'cause he's dead!" Dub replied.

"Well, let me call Damar right quick." Boo Boo dialed him.

"What up, Boo Boo?"

"Yo, bruh, somebody hit the stash house. All the money gone."

"Fuck! Gone? Gone where? I told y'all niggas to be careful! Yo, check this out. Collect the money from Oga and I want all of y'all to fly back to L.A. I got something I gotta tell you guys," Damar said.

"Alright, see you in a couple of hours."

Big Boo Boo and Dub-Sac met up with Oga in Miami at one of their warehouses and collected the money. Taz couldn't be reached so Damar told them to fly back without him. He assumed Taz was handling some business and he would call when he could.

While Damar was waiting on his crew. He was lying in bed with baby Prince on his chest asleep. He hadn't called Sunja yet because he was debating if he should tell Jamerica about her. His old way of thinking said, *fuck calling Sunja and don't tell Jamerica shit*. But his new mind frame told him he needed closure if he wanted a clear conscious. Another hour had passed and after thinking long and hard, he made his decision.

He gently laid the baby next to Jamerica and then stepped in the kitchen area. He called Sunja three times and each time it went straight to voicemail. Apparently, she had her phone turned off. He didn't leave a message, he was just going to try again later.

He went back into the bedroom and sat beside Jamerica. He rubbed her smooth back and her eyes slowly came unglued and she round over.

A beautiful smile appeared on her face. "Hello, my king." They laced their hands together,

"Hey, baby, how you feeling?"

"I feel good, I'm just tired."

"Baby, I got something to tell you. Well actually two things," Damar said.

Jamerica slowly sat up against the headboard. "I think I know about one of them. I went through your phone while you were sleep."

"Why you do that? You ain't never rambled through my phone," Damar said in disbelief.

Jamerica crossed her arms. "You a man, ain't cha? I been gone almost a year and I know how you like to fuck. So, where is this Sunja hoe at?"

Damar sighed. "She at a hotel in Arizona."

"Why is she at a hotel? Is she waiting on you?"

"Kinda sorta."

"What the fuck does that mean? Either she is or she ain't." Jamerica snapped.

"Yeah, she's waiting on me." Damar admitted.

"So that's who you want?"

"Naw, baby, I tried to call her a minute ago and tell her that it was over, but she didn't answer the phone. It's you I want in my life, baby."

Jamerica huffed. “Try it again, right now and put it on speaker.”

“Cool,” Damar said and hit redial. Again, it went straight to voicemail.

“We’ll try it again later,” Jamerica said with prominence. “Okay, what else did you have to tell me?”

Damar then cupped her hands and gazed into her eyes. “I’m getting out the game, for good this time. You and Prince are worth more than this crazy life. I don’t ever want to put your life in jeopardy again. And my son is going to make something out of himself. I’ma make sure he will never know what’s behind his daddy’s footsteps. That’s why we’re leaving the country.

Jamerica shrugged her shoulders. “Where we going?”

“Where do you wanna go?”

Jamerica raised her eyebrows and squeezed his hands. “How about Italy?”

“Italy it is, shawty.”

“Can we go now?” Jamerica asked ready to leave.

“I’m waiting on the crew, they should be here in a couple of hours. They have money. I’ma break them off and then we’ll leave, okay?

“Okay,” Jamerica said and then they embraced for a moment.

When Damar released his gentle hold, he rubbed the side of her face, “I’ma hop in the shower right quick, okay?”

Jamerica smiled. “Yeah do that. I thought I smelled something.”

Damar sniffed under his armpit. “Nah, that’s your upper lip.” When Jamerica went to hit him, he struck out to the bathroom laughing.

Jamerica shook her head and looked down at baby Prince. He was sucking on his finger. She leaned over and started baby talking to him. "Give me some of that finger."

When she finished playing with him, somebody popped up in her head. So she eased out of bed and grabbed Damar's phone off the night stand and dialed a number. The phone rang two times before someone answered.

"Hello?" The voice said.

Jamerica didn't recognize the voice. "Who is this?"

"You called this phone. Who are you?"

"Oh, I'm sorry this is Jamerica. Is Tamika around?"

"Nah, Tamika was killed a couple of months ago. I'm her niece."

Jamerica stopped breathing and covered her mouth. When she exhaled she slowly walked over to the bed and sat down. "Oh, my God. What happened?"

"Somebody came in her apartment and stabbed her to death." She sat on the phone for a minute listening to Jamerica cry her eyes out. Then she heard the phone hit the floor and the call disconnected.

When Damar walked out of the bathroom, he saw Jamerica crying. He rushed over and gently touched her back. "Baby, what's wrong?"

It was seconds before she turned to him and wiped her face. Her voice trembled, "Why did you do it? Why, baby, why? Why did you have to kill Tamika?"

Seeing his girl in that emotional state almost brought tears to his own eyes. He knew if he admitted to having Tamika murdered he would be driving the stake deeper into her broken heart. So he lied to protect it. He calmly sat next to her and continued to caress her back. He tried to look and sound sincere as possible, "Baby, I had nothing to do with it." He stared into her saddened eyes.

Jamerica wiped her nose and looked in his face for the truth. All she saw was pain, but she couldn't tell if it was from guilt or sympathy. So she wrapped her arms around him and held on real tight. "Damar, I know you did it." She cried.

"Baby, I…"

"I'm just ready to go!" Jamerica screamed.

Damar didn't want to make it any worse so he shut up and rubbed the back of her head. "As soon as they bring me my money, we're gonna leave, baby. Just be patient."

Chapter 18
Lakeview Condominiums
An hour ago

As soon as Taz zipped his Gucci bag, the door bell rung. In a hurry, he grabbed his bag and headed for the door. Whoever it was, they were going to have to talk to him on the way to his car if he was going to make his flight to L.A.

When he opened the door, he dropped his bag when he saw a man standing there in what looked to be a disguise. He had on a black trench coat, black gloves, a Stetson hat and shades. The man flashed a gun and ushered him back inside and locked the door.

"What the bumba clot?" Taz asked as he back stepped. The man took his shades off and put them in his pocket.

Taz became angry. "Why are you here? I thought you died?"

The man chuckled, "It's check out time, nigga. Your services are no longer needed."

"Bullshit! Damar called me about an hour ago," Taz said.

Fresh lowered his brow and brandished his gun. "You lying piece of shit. He's dead, they all dead! If he's alive, call him. Call him now, muthafucka!"

Taz slowly put his hand insides his coat and made contact with his phone. As he was attempting to pull it out, his hand brushed across his steel in his shoulder holster. *I can take him,* he thought and released the phone and grabbed his .38 revolver.

Fresh got his shot off first.

Blocka! Blocka!

He hit Taz in the stomach twice. Taz dropped to one knee and managed to get a shot off. A single slug ripped clean through Fresh's thigh. He stumbled back against the wall.

Once he got his balance he hopped over to finish Taz off. Suddenly he heard a lot of commotion stirring outside. He glanced down at his leg and he started feeling light headed when he saw all the blood jetting out of his leg. He panicked and ran out the door and jumped in his getaway car. A green Chevy caprice he'd bought earlier from a street dealer.

Taz' neighbor, Mr. Curry, rushed inside of the condo after Fresh fled the scene. Mr. Curry was an old frail white man. He barely had enough strength to help Taz on the sofa. Taz moaned in agony, he felt his life slipping away. He fumbled for his phone and scrolled down his call log and hit send. It rang three times before Damar answered.

"Yo, what up, Taz?"

"Aha, Fresh. Alive. He just shot me," he said, dropping the phone.

Mr. Curry grabbed the phone and told Damar that Taz was dead.

***

Los Angeles California

When Damar's crew arrived at the hotel, he took them into the living room. Big Boo Boo laid two brief cases full of money on the table, then he took a seat on the couch next to Oga and Dub-Sac.

Damar walked over to the table wearing a grey suit and black loafers. He opened the brief cases and examined the money. He then began to count out $100,000 to give to each of them.

While Damar was handing out the money, Big Boo Boo noticed the disarray on Damar's face. "Yo, what's up, bruh? What this meeting about?"

Damar looked at everyone before answering Boo Boo's question. "Yo, up until the other day I wanted to stay in the game forever and die a *G*. I really didn't give a fuck about nothing or nobody but myself. But when I looked into my son's eyes, that vision went away. I saw me and Jamerica living a normal life, raising our son the right way together."

"So what you saying, bruh? Boo Boo asked.

Oga raised his hand, "Who's gonna run the cartel?

"Nobody! The King Cartel ends with me. But I got one more thing I gotta do before I leave the country for good. Y'all can roll with me this one last time or I can do it alone."

"You know we riding wit'cha no matter what it is. So what's up?" Dub-Sac asked.

"Fresh still alive. He killed Taz."

"Damn," Boo Boo rubbed his hand over his head.

Oga and Dub-Sac just remained silent. The sadness was evident on Oga's face.

"Okay, since everybody's down, we gotta find that nigga," Damar said.

"I'll have one of my boys go by his house in Miami and see if he's there." Oga called him up.

Thirty minutes later, Oga's boy called back and said that some white chick was at Fresh's residence. Along with a picture message of her getting out of a red Mercedes.

Oga relayed the message to Damar and showed him the picture.

"That bitch still alive!" Damar yelled, eyeballing the photo with resentment.

"Yo, Boo Boo, charter us a plane. I gotta tell Jamerica our trip will be delayed."

"I'm on it, bruh," Boo Boo replied as Damar got up and took the brief cases to the back.

Chapter 19

Eight p.m. Miami Florida. East 21st

"Oh fuck!" That shit hurts." Fresh cried out as he laid on the couch while Cassie tended to his wound. She was alive and well. Fresh couldn't bring himself to kill her. Instead he told her what Damar wanted him to do to her. Then Cassie came up with the idea to fake her death and all it took to deceive Damar was a little make-up and ketchup.

"Be still, I gotta put clean bandages on it or it might get gangrene."

"Ah! Well, hurry the fuck up!" Fresh yelled and turned up the fifth of vodka that was almost gone.

When Cassie finish cleaning his leg, he asked to see her phone. She grabbed it off the coffee table and handed it to him and then plopped next to him on the couch. As Fresh hit the screen, she leaned over and asked "What are you doing?"

Fresh finished what he was doing and then handed her the phone. She looked at the screen. He had saved a bank address and some numbers.

"What is this?" she asked

Fresh faced her. "It an account number, just in case something happens to me, you'll be straight."

Cassie shook her head, "What do you mean? Is there something you're not telling me?"

Not to worry, her Fresh lied. "Nah, baby, I'm good. It's a *just in case* thing."

Cassie nodded that she understood, then asked. "Well, how much is in it?"

Fresh grinned. "More than we can count."

Cassie squinted her eyes and giggled. "What did you do? Rob a bank?"

Fresh laughed, “Ha, ha, ha, hell nah. baby. You know I don’t steal. I took it.”

Cassie sat up and crossed her legs. She was just about to ask him who did he take it from but then the doorbell rang.

Fresh’s head snapped. “You expecting somebody?” He asked paranoid, wondering if Damar was really still alive.

Cassie shook her head. “No, I’ll go see who it is.”

“Look through the peep hole first.” Fresh yelled.

Cassie spun around with her hand on her hip. “No shit.” First, she looked in the peep hole then opened the door.

“Who the fuck is it?” Fresh yelled again.

“It’s the mailman,” Cassie replied.

It was a tall light skin brother wearing a USPS uniform with hazel eyes.

She had on a blue halter-top and a pair of white boy-shorts that were sucked into her coochie. She met his lustful gaze and put on her sexy voice. “Hi, can I help you.”

“Hello, I have a package for Cassie King.”

Cassie smiled and sprung on her tip toes. “That’s me!”

“Alright here you go.” He handed her the box, then pulled out a clipboard and pen. “Sign here, please.”

Cassie took the pen, signed her name and glanced back at the Heisman trophy in front of her. She gently took the post-man’s hand and wrote her phone number in his palm.

When she looked up, he mumbled, “Damn, what a waste.” He shook his head.

“Call me.” She mouthed and eased the door shut. On the way to the kitchen, she shook the box. “I wonder what it is.”

“Shit, you ordered it didn’t you?” Fresh asked sarcastically before securing the front door. Then he walked toward the kitchen curious to know what was in the package. “What is it?” He asked upon entering the elaborate kitchen with stainless steel appliances.

Cassie had just opened the box. It was a digital device mounted on a piece of Styrofoam. Cassie froze up and held her breath. Fresh saw the disillusion on her face and asked as he looked over her shoulder. “Cassie! What the fuck is it?”

She slowly turned to him with a petrified look on her face. “I think it’s a—”

Boom! Boom! Boom!

Chapter 20

When Damar heard the big explosion over the phone, he felt better knowing he had Fresh killed. Then he told the fake postman to check his account and in fifteen minutes because the one hundred bands would be there.

He and his crew were flying high above the clouds heading to Jersey. He figured he might as well handle all personal business before leaving the country.

Prior to having Fresh and Cassie blown to hell, Damar hired another hit man to eliminate Mo the last survivor on Dub-Sac's hit list.

He was an independent assassin named Carlos but where he was from was unknown. But he was highly recommend by Ricardo. He was said to be one of the best in the business. So while Damar was on his way to deal with his stock broker, Tom Prath, for running off with his money, Carlos was in Monroe, Georgia parked outside of the Hardy's restaurant, where Mo worked part-time from 5 to 9 p.m. as an assistant manager. All of that and a full description of Mo was stated on his assignment sheet, that he got from Damar.

The night air was cool, flowing through the cracked window. Carlos was comfortable behind the limousine tint in his black F-150. He felt invisible dressed in all-black, while listening to symphony music. He checked the time on his watch, it was twenty minutes after nine. By his calculations, Mo should be coming out of the restaurant at any minute. Another minute passed before Mo's wide body came out and walked to his gold Expedition.

"Son of a bitch." Mo huffed when he saw his front tire was flat. He opened the driver's side door and tossed his briefcase on the seat and slammed the door, then he walked to the rear and popped the hatchback. He grabbed the jack and spare tire and headed back to the front of the vehicle.

Across the parking lot, Carlos slipped on his Isotone gloves and retrieved a black box from the passenger seat. He opened it and gently ran his hand over the weapon. Then he carefully took it out of the box and assembled it. Then he put one in the chamber, screwed on the silencer and eased the window down.

By this time Mo had unloosened the lugs and was now jacking the vehicle up, Carlos scanned the lot. It was clear, so he carefully took aim and put Mo's head between the cross-hairs. The symphony music was still harmonizing to Carlos's mind. He liked this song because the instruments played with suspense. Every time he heard it, it gave him an adrenaline rush and made him want to kill. When it got to the part where it sounded like a hundred violins stringing the same note, Carlos pulled the trigger. The bullet slammed into the back of Mo's skull and everything in his head splattered on the tire and fender, then his lifeless body fell on the side of the truck.

Chapter 21

The plane landed in Newark at 10 p.m. From there, Damar rented a black 2015 Camaro and drove to Tom Prath's farm house on Montgomery Road. The entrance was gated with a long driveway leading up to Tom's huge white house. The house was surrounded by a white stone wall.

Damar got his number from Tom's old secretary where he used to work.

A light flipped off upstairs, so that confirmed there was someone home.

Everyone was dressed in all-black. Boo Boo was driving and Damar was on the passenger side, Dub-Sac and Oga crammed in the back.

"Yo, Boo Boo, park on the other side of the road behind that old barn. Don't look like too much traffic come down this road. We gonna be in and out once I put a bullet in this cracker's head." Damar put on his gloves and ski-mask. His crew did likewise and they jumped out of the car. Once they reached the property line, Boo Boo deactivated the alarm system. Then they all climbed over the privacy wall.

***

Tom was in his home office kicked back on his tan recliner talking to a client. His conversation was interrupted by his wife's Pomeranian, Sam. He was barking in the foyer adjacent to the office.

"Hold on, Gary." Tom put the phone down and massaged his temples. "Hey, Jennifer! Will you shut that damn dog up?"

Damar and his crew were standing in the foyer when Sam ran up and started tugging on Dub-Sac's leg.

Damar grabbed Sam by the skin on his neck and held him up. Sam snarled and bared his teeth at him.

Damar got nose to nose with him and growled, "Grrrrrr!"

Sam started whimpering and peed on the floor.

Tom's wife walked in at that same moment with green rollers in her hair wearing pink lingerie that probably used to fit once upon a time. She had rolls of fat hanging over her panty line, a flat ass and her stretch marked titties looked like deflated balloons. They couldn't tell what her face looked like because she had on a beauty mask.

When she went to scream, Dub-Sac threw his Glock in her face. "One note come out and I'ma blow out your speakers, bitch!" She quickly covered her mouth with both hands and Damar handed her the dog.

"Jennifer, can you bring me a glass of water?" Tom yelled. Then he continued his phone call.

"Yeah, Gary, I'm the best in the business, check my credentials." Tom bragged and let out a melodramatic laugh.

"If you knew how stupid you sound, you would never laugh again." Damar walked in the room and removed his ski mask.

Tom dropped his phone and damn near jumped through the roof. "Wh—what in heavens?"

"The only thing you need to be praying for is that I make this shit quick," Damar shoved Jennifer next to him. "Get your bad body ass over there with your shit eating husband."

Jennifer wobbled over with Sam wedged between her breast. "Oh, Tom, what's going on?"

"Tell her, Tom. Tell the misses how you shitted me out my stocks."

Tom's voice came out cracked. "No, Carl, it was nothing like that. I had to change my number for legal reasons."

"You had my number." Damar reminded him.

"I—I lost it." Tom stuttered. "Honestly, I did. I looked for it everywhere. Didn't I, Jenn?"

His wife nodded in correspondence.

Damar narrowed his eyes and pulled his Glock from his waist. "As a democrat, Tom, I don't believe shit a republican says."

Tom fell to his knees and started begging for his life. "No, no, no, Carl, please! I'll give it back to you. I'll even give you double. Just don't kill me, please! Please! My only son is graduating from college this fall. Please! When I found out you were on America's Most Wanted, I had to cut all ties with you to protect my family, Carl. What extreme would you go to, to protect yours?"

When Tom mentioned family Damar grew less tense. He thought about what Tom was saying. Here he was giving up everything he and his brother built for Jamerica and Prince. And Tom was a man that loved his family just as much as he did. So he couldn't kill him for that. He lowered his gun and put it back in his waistline.

He walked over to the desk grabbed a pen and jotted some numbers down on a piece of paper. "You got twenty-four hours to send double of what my stocks were worth to this account."

"Oh, thank you, Carl. Thank you. It will be there by noon tomorrow." Tom promised.

Jennifer put Sam down and ran into Tom's arms. "Oh, Tom, you're such a brave man."

Dub-Sac shook his head and laughed. "Hee, hee, hee, what movie dis hoe watching."

Damar slid his mask back on. "Just so you know, I got a backup crew that will come back and kill your whole family. So don't be stupid and call the police when I leave."

Tom squeezed his wife's shoulder. "I understand. No calls."

"Good!" Damar led his crew out the house.

Chapter 22

By the time they reached their car, it started thundering and then came the lighting followed by heavy rain. When they got to the small airport on the outskirts of Jersey, the storm worsened. Their flight was delayed until the rain storm passed. They sat in the parking lot for thirty minutes waiting. In between time, Damar called to check on Jamerica and the baby. Prince was fine but Jamerica wasn't. She was impatiently waiting to leave the country. Damar told her that he had handled his business and was just waiting on the storm to clear. But it still didn't make her feel any better. Damar listened to her whine and bitch for another five minutes before they got off of the phone.

"Man, it's hard to please a woman." Damar watched the rain pound the windshield.

Boo Boo had just got off of the phone with Sandy. She was missing the hell out her teddy bear, but she was more understanding then Jamerica was.

Oga was asleep and Dub was listening to some music on his phone.

"Rain coming down hard," Boo Boo said.

Damar nodded, then he laid his head back on the headrest and let out an exasperating breathe. "Man, I need a drink."

"And I need some food." Boo Boo replied, rubbing his stomach.

"I'ight, lets ride. We'll come back when the storm clears."

***

Big Boo Boo drove up the Jersey shore and found a parking space in front of a bar called Riley's Pub.

Dub-Sac nudged Oga to wake up. Oga sat up and glanced out of the window. It was still pouring down. The sidewalks were illuminated by the colorful building lights. People were scurrying with umbrellas and newspapers over their heads.

"Yo, fellas, I wanna say something before we go inside. I know I don't say it much, but I really 'preciate your contribution to The Cartel. Y'all some real solid niggas. And if I had to do it all over again, I would want y'all right there by my side. I'm gonna miss the hell out of y'all, I aint gon' lie. So this last drink with y'all is going to be special. One I will never forget for as long as I live. And that's on everything." Damar noticed everyone had the sad face.

To him that meant he was going to be missed too. He grinned and cleared his throat. "C'mon, let's get our drink on before y'all start crying on a nigga."

Chapter 23

Riley's was filled to capacity. The crowd was mixed. It had one long bar with ten female bartender's. They all had on black tank tops and white jeans.

There was a silk banister above the stage that read: Comedy Night.

"Yeah just what I need, a few drinks and a good laugh," Damar said and then he and his boys walked across the red carpet to a table.

A waitress was at their service before they could sit down. She quickly took their orders and dashed away like she had on rocket skates. Then the spotlight hit the stage, it was time for the next comic.

The host of the show introduced him as Phil Ray from Brooklyn, New York. Phil was black and skinny and was one of the best at making funny faces, which made his jokes more hilarious. Phil had sleepy eyes, buck teeth and a nappy ass head. He looked like a cross between Pooky from New Jack City and Sammy Davis Jr. Phil hopped on stage accompanied by his theme song *No Games* by Rick Ross, doing the old school dance *the cabbage patch.* His long neck went from left to right. His scrawny shoulders looked like a wire cloths hanger under his shirt.

"Hee, hee, hee. Dis nigga bettta be funny or I'ma shoot his ass right off stage," Boo Boo chuckled.

"Me too, my nigga."

"Me tree, mi bruda." Oga laughed.

"Ha, ha! Yeah, we'll swiss cheese his Brooklyn ass." Damar joked.

When the music stopped, Phil Ray adjusted the mic, then he went into his act.

"That's right, Phil Ray, don't play no games with these hoes. I speak my mother fuckin' mind. I had a fat hoe once." He paused. "Don't y'all niggas be looking at me like I'm a terrorist and I'm about to blow this bitch up. I'm pretty sure all y'all done had a big girl before. But anyway, she was big, no fuck that, the bitch was huuge! You hear me. I remember one time she fell out in the middle of the street. I called an ambulance. When they got there, them muthafuckers called a tow truck. They hooked her big ass up by her draws and hauled ass."

The crowd was in stitches. There was a fat lady on the front row wearing a patent leather body suit laughing so hard she fell out of her seat and flopped on the floor.

The spotlight beamed down on her. "Get yo fat ass up, coming up in here looking like a baby seal." Then he mimicked a seal. "Uh! Uh! Uh!"

The crowd went wild again. Damar even had to laugh on that one.

When the noise ceased, Phil Ray went on with his act. "Okay, the second fat chick I had was cute as hell. But her body looked like a Volkswagen. This was around the time when I sold crack cocaine. But I used it on special occasions. But anyway her name was Big Mary. I'll never forget Big Mary. I used to get lost between them big ass thighs, I felt like a needle in a haystack. What I liked about Big Mary was she was determined to lose weight. Bitch drank a case of slim-fast a day, but that shit didn't work. So I put her on the crack-head diet. That stem-fast, where you smoke all the shake and lose the weight." Phil got another round of applause and closed out his act. "Now that bitch can stand behind a stop sign and you wouldn't see her." Phil laughed and bowed. "Thanks, y'all been great. I'm Phil Ray. Peace!"

While Damar and his crew were waiting on the next act, the waitress finally showed up with their drinks. No one noticed her mouth twitching but Dub-Sac. She was geeked up off coke or meth. He wasn't sure which one. When she left the table, Dub-Sac waited a minute, then he went looking for her.

Big Boo Boo was so hungry he forgot his manners and started ripping his grilled leg quarters apart, "Um. Um. Um!"

Oga laughed, "Do you eat pussy de same way?"

Boo Boo held his head up still chomping away. He smiled. "Ask ya girl, nigga."

Damar snickered and sipped his Martini. *Shaken not stirred.*

"Ha,ha,ha, funny," Oga grinned.

"Yo, Damar, I been thinking about getting out the game, too. And invest my money in a barber shop or something I don't know yet," Boo Boo said with a mouth full of food.

"That's what's up, big homie. That's a good investment. What Sandy say about it?"

"I hadn't told her yet. I'ma surprise her when I get home. Then I'ma give her this." Boo Boo reached in his pocket and pulled out a black box.

"What's in it? Oga asked.

"A ring nigga, what you think?" Boo Boo replied all jovial.

"Aha, hope she likes it," Olga said.

"For twenty thousand dollars she better love it."

"Ha, ha, I know that shit right, Boo Boo," Damar said.

***

Dub-Sac purposely ran into the waitress when he saw her spring from the back. She dropped the tray she had in her hand. "Damn, my bad, shawty." Dub apologized and helped her clean up the mess.

"No, I'm sorry, I wasn't watching where I was going." She was geeked out of her mind. Her eyes were so big it looked like they would pop if touched. Her head bobbled as she spoke and she sounded like a robot. Then she wiped the clear snot from her upper lip with the back of her hand.

"Shawty, you fucked up, ain't cha?"

She glanced around and touched her lips, "Is it that noticeable?"

Hee, hee, hee. Shawty, you look like a raw chicken running around this muthafucka."

She frowned. "Oh, my God, that bad?"

"Yeah, but it's all good. I'm trying to get high, too. What you on?"

"A little coke, meth, weed and pills."

"Dub-Sac stopped her," Hey, hey, I just want some coke. I got plenty of money."

"I think I got about two grams left."

"A'ight, let me try it out. You got somewhere we can duck off?"

"Yeah, I do, wait! She paused. "You're not a killer or anything are you?" She whispered.

Dub-Sac laughed. "Yeah, I'ma hit-man for a cartel."

She tilted her head and saw the smirk on his face. Then she wiped her nose again and burst out laughing. "That's a good one." What's your name anyway?" She asked and put the tray on the counter.

"Mic." Dub replied.

"Okay, I'm Julie, nice to meet you."

"You too, so what's up?"

"Alright listen, we'll do it this way so nobody won't see us. Down the hall and on your left." She pointed. "There's a janitor's closet, meet me there in five minutes."

Dub nodded. "That's what's up."

Chapter 24

Five minutes later, Dub tapped on the janitor's door. Julie cracked the door and then pulled him inside. The closet smelled like dirty mop water. There were mops, brooms, and other cleaning supplies hanging on the yellow wall.

Julie dispersed a bunch of junk out her purse onto the sink. She rummaged through it until she found the cocaine in a clear baggy. She ripped the bag and poured the contents on her make-up mirror. She chalked out four long lines and snorted one with a straw. She then handed it to Dub-Sac.

First he took his finger and tested the drug to make sure it was only cocaine. It was, so he sniffed a line. "Ahhh, dis some good shit," he said when he felt the burn. Then he handed the straw back to Julie. She started sniffing crazy. Dub then snatched the straw, "My turn, shawty, you got a mean vacuum cleaner."

Julie giggled, "You're funny as shit. You called my nose a vacuum cleaner!" After Dub hit the line, Julie lifted her shirt "Look! This is what good coke does to me." Her nipples were hard. "It gets me horny as fuck." She squeezed her titties.

Dub wiped his nose. "Shiiit you feel like sucking some dick?"

"Oh, I love sucking dick, as long as it ain't a small one."

"Ain't nothing little about me, but my patience." Dub dropped his pants to his ankles. Julie's eyes got bigger than they already were.

"Oh, my God, is that fuckin' real?" She touched it. She pulled on it twice and Dub got harder. Then Julie leaned over and Dub grabbed the back of her head and pushed his mule dick in her tiny mouth.

"Um, um, um, she hummed and gagged when she tried to swallow too much. She spit his dick out, caught her breath and then she tried it again. This time she acted like she had some sense and not like a greedy ass hoe.

“Ummm ummm ummm.” She moaned. Julie was enjoying herself. But Dub wasn’t too thrilled about her teeth scratching his dick. He wanted to nut but he couldn’t take no more. It felt like his dick was bleeding.

He stopped her with his hand, “Hold up, shawty. You carving my wood with them beaver teeth, let me see what that pussy hitting like.”

“Oh, it’s nice and tight.” She took off her jeans. She had skinny legs and a little butt. Her white thongs looked like a baby’s shoe string. “You got a condom?”

“Naw, I’m clean. You good?” Dub asked while stroking himself.

Julie stuck her finger in her pussy and licked it. “Finger licking!”

“I bet it is, but I don’t eat no pussy. Just bend yo ass over.”

Julie bent over and braced the sink and glanced to the side. “Hey, Mic, go easy back there.”

Dub-Sac pulled her little panties to the side, grabbed her tiny waist and slid in raw dog. She was super tight. He slowly penetrated her and he felt her walls stretching.

“Oh, my God! Oh, my fucking, God! That shit hurts like hell!” Julie stood there and took it.

“Oh, yeah! Ohhhh yeah!” Dub moaned as he sped up.

When he finally broke her walls in, her pussy got wet as SeaWorld. Then he started ramming her. His pelvis smashed against her narrow butt cheeks and he was seconds away from cumming.

Julie was screaming like a monkey. “Uh! Uh! I, I, Uh! Uh! I, I!”

Then Dub took one hard thrust and filled her pussy with cum. Julie was glad when he stopped and pulled his pants up.

She hurried up and put her jeans back on before he went for seconds.

"Fuck, when was the last time you had some?" She held her stomach.

Dub ignored her and started on the last line of coke. By the time Julie slipped on her shirt, all the dope was gone.

"Mic! Did you have to do it all?" She pouted.

Dub was high and forgot he told her that was his name. He looked at her like she was crazy. "Who's Mic?"

"Dude, you're fucking high." she laughed. "You forgot your own name."

Dub shook his head. "You crazy. Say, can you get some more of this shit?"

"Hell, fuck, yeah. But it's expensive, though."

"I need an ounce," Dub said with a serious look on his face.

She returned the stare. "You got that much money?"

Dub went in his pocket and pulled out a bank roll. "Bitch, do it look like I'm broke, what's the ticket?"

Julie shrugged her shoulders "I don't know. I only buy an eight-ball at a time."

"Um, it's some good grade but it can't cost no more than twenty five hundred. Plug me in, shawty, take me to the man."

"I can't do that, he's funny about people he don't know."

All of a sudden, Dub-Sac started feeling the full effects of the coke. His mouth began twitching, he had the jones. "Well, how far you gotta go to get it?"

"He's here, he owns the place."

"What color is he?" Dub asked.

Julie smiled, "He's blue."

Dub didn't smile or blink.

"Okay, okay, I was just kidding. Carlos is Italian."

"Yo, check dis out, shawty. As you can see I got the money, but I'ma give you a five hundred now and when you bring me my shit, I'll give you the rest."

Julie thought for a second, "Umm. No, I know Carlos and he won't do it that way."

"Damn," Dub quickly counted out ten one hundred dollar bills and handed it to her. "Listen, shawty, you know where my table at. When you get the coke, bring me a beer and that will be my signal to meet you back here."

"Alright give me at least thirty minutes." Julie put the money in her apron. She went for the door. Dub grabbed her arm "Thirty minutes, don't make me come looking for you."

Julie smiled. "Thirty minutes, I got you."

Chapter 25

When Dub-Sac came back to the table, the crowd was simmering down. A comedian just left the stage.

"What up, Dub? You missed it. Olé boy was funny as a muthafucka," Boo Boo chuckled as he leaned back in his chair full as a tick.

Oga was still clapping. "That was good."

Damar cut his eyes at Dub. He could tell he was high. "Yo, Dub, what are your plans for the future?" Damar asked, eating the olive off of the toothpick from his dirty martini.

Dub rubbed his nose. "Shit, I might start my own cartel. What you think?"

"To each his own, my nigga. If that's what you wanna do, go for it," Damar said right when the host of the show walked back on stage.

"Everybody put your hands together for the sexy, funny and talented Mary Jane from Charleston, South Carolina."

The crowd gave her a warm welcome as she walked on stage in a pair of white jeans and a Golden State basketball jersey. Her hair was micro braided to the back and she had an inviting smile. She waved to the crowd until the cheering stopped.

"How's everybody doing tonight?" She asked, taking the microphone off of the stand. The crowd gave her another round of applause.

"That's good, I see some ballers came out tonight. But hell that don't do me no good because I don't work for tips." She looked over the crowd.

"Oh shit! Is that Donald Trump sitting in the corner?" She said, pointing to the guy who resembled the rich mogul.

The spotlight turned on him. Once Mary Jane got a better look, she started clowning on the man. "Oh, hell nah. He too damn short." His feet don't even touch the floor. Look at his little midget legs justa swinging. The man turned red when everyone started laughing at him. "Okay, okay, that wasn't a part of my act. Stick to the script, Mary Jane, and leave Mini Trump alone." The crowd laughed again.

"Okay some of y'all know me and some of y'all don't. My name is Mary Jane and yes it's my real name. My father named me after his drug of choice. Which may sound bad, but it's not because I could've been named after my mother's drug of choice, which was crack cocaine.

"Yeah. Think about how my first day of school could've been. Imagine the teacher calling roll call." Mary Jane quickly put on a pair of bifocals that made her eyes appear extra-large. Then she held out an imaginary piece of paper and pretended that she was reading it.

"Crack cocaine!" She said in a winey voice. Then she looked over the rim of her glasses as if peering around a real classroom. "Crack Cocaine, can you please raise your hand" The crowd burst out laughing. Mary Jane smiled and removed the glasses.

"Whoa. Is it hot in here or is it me?" Mary Jane said, fanning her face. "I feel like I'm in a damn incubator. My eggs in my ovaries are probably boiled. Shit! Got me sweating like a nigga sitting in an electric chair. Can a bitch get a fan?"

Suddenly Damar's phone rang, it was Sunja. He picked up on the third ring. "Hey, Sunja," he said dryly.

"Oh, baby! I couldn't wait any longer, I had to call. Are you okay? Where are you?"

"I'm good, I made it back safely." Sunja got silent, she felt something was wrong. Damar didn't sound enthused like she was. "You're going to be with her aren't you?"

"Listen, Sunja, I love you but—"

"Say no more." She cut him off. Her voice was weak and her heart ached. It felt like someone was ringing it out like a wet rag. Damar could hear her gasping for air on the other end. She didn't know he was hurting inside, too. He really wished there was another way, but there wasn't.

"Bruh, what's up?" Boo Boo asked.

Damar cupped the phone, "I'm good." He whispered. Then he got back on the line. "Sunja, will you hear me out first?"

"No, Damar! Save your poor excuses. Fuck you and her! Oh and just so you know, I just decided to have an abortion."

Click!

"Sunja! Sunja!" Damar yelled into the phone. When he saw that she had hung up, he tried to call her back but her phone was off.

Damar buried his head in his arms on the table. *Damn she was pregnant.*

A minute later his phone rang. He quickly answered it.

"Hello, Sunja?"

"Dis ain't no damn Sunja!"

"Oh, shit! Jamerica, baby."

"Don't baby me, muthafucka. What you can't find the bitch?" *Click!*

"Muthafucka!" Damar slammed his fist on the table out of frustration.

"Yo, bruh, want me to check on the plane?" Boo Boo asked.

"Yeah, see what's up?" Damar replied and called Jamerica two more times, but she wouldn't pick up.

Dub-Sac checked his watch. It was time for Julie to pop up at any moment. He glanced around the place, there was no sign of her. He grew inpatient and got up from the table, "Yo, I'ma run to the bathroom."

"I'ight hurry back, we 'bout to be out," Damar said.

Someone at the airport finally answered the phone as soon as Dub left. Boo Boo spoke briefly and ended the call. "The plane's ready." He nodded at Damar.

"Cool, we'll dip when Dub get back from the men's room."

***

Dub-Sac combed through the place for fifteen minutes. There was no trace of Julie. His phone kept lighting up, it was Damar calling him to see what was taking him so long. He ignored it and kept searching and anyone blocking his path, he shoved out of the way. When he got tired of running in circles he snatched a waitress up by the arm. His grip was tight and his pupils were dilated, he was sweating.

"Hey, bitch, you seen Julie?" Dub-Sac was pressing against her funny bone.

"Ouch! Julie clocked out twenty minutes ago." The woman cried.

"What? Bitch, don't lie to me." Dub said as he jerked her back and forth.

A bouncer saw Dub-Sac shaking the waitress like a rag-doll and rushed over and clobbered him in the face. Dub fell on the floor then two other bouncers came over and started kicking him. He folded up to avoid getting his teeth knocked out. The fight caused an uproar in the bar. People were on the sideline rooting for the bouncer. From afar Damar could see that someone was getting the shit stomped out of them by security.

Boo Boo had a better look from the angle he was sitting. "That's Dub!" He ran to his rescue. He clotheslined one of the men.

Damar and Oga came up a second later and started brawling with the other two.

Dub-Sac was then able to crawl under a table. His neck and back was in a lot of pain. It hurt like hell but he endured the pain and retrieved his Glock from his leg holster. Once he gripped the steel, he felt a sense of urgency. He cocked his weapon and flipped the table over and started dumping. He took out the bouncers first then he shot a few more people just on G.P.

When Dub finished shooting, Damar yelled, "Let's get the fuck outta here!" And they fled from the scene, hopped in their ride and headed for the airport.

As Damar weaved through traffic, everybody was trying to talk at the same time. "Hey, hey everybody shut the fuck up!" Damar yelled.

Everyone became silent, all that could be heard was the windshield wipers going back and forth.

"Dub! What the fuck was that all about?" Damar asked.

"Bruh, ain't did shit. Them muthafuckas jumped me." Dub said, peering out the side window.

Damar kept his focus on the road as he thought to himself. *Man, I'm so glad this shit finna be over with. I ain't never coming back.*

Chapter 26

Damar drove with precaution for two miles and had to make a sudden stop at the red light. He was unaware that a cop had just whipped behind him. Someone reported the car and tag number when they fled from Riley's Pub, so all units within a ten mile radius were on the lookout for a black Camaro with chrome wheels, license plate 756KO.

Whoop! Whoop! Whoop!

The cop flipped on his lights after confirming the plates.

"Fuck!" Damar said when he saw the lights in the rear-view. He didn't have to second guess on what to do. He stiff armed the steering wheel and punched the accelerator. The tires spun. The car went out of control and fish tailed into on-coming traffic. Damar then put the vehicle in reverse, it did a one-eighty spin and crashed into the guard rail. He heard a horn and looked up at a Mack truck coming full speed ahead in their direction. "Oh shit!" He put the car in drive and stomped the gas. The car jolted back into traffic and the semi barely missed the bumper. The vibration shook the whole car.

The squad car gave chase and within minutes there were twenty police cars on their trail. Dub-Sac turned and shot the back window out and started shooting. Oga reached under the seat and grabbed a Tech 9 and joined him.

They busted the first squad car's radiator, and the car crashed into another vehicle. One by one, Dub and Oga were knocking them off like flies. But more kept coming from every junction.

The Camaro was fast so each car that got close enough tried to ram them but each attempt Damar dodged them. He was handling the street machine like he was a NASCAR driver.

Boo Boo finally found his Glock that had slid up under the seat. He opened fire on the cars on the passenger side and he happened to look up in the sky. “Bruh, they got the Ghetto bird on us,” he said when he saw the news helicopter. He quickly reloaded and started firing at the chopper. The Glock had no accuracy. The helicopter was too high in the air.

Up ahead, Damar spotted smog. He hit the fog lights and the Camaro vanished into the cloudlike mist. Then he dropped the car in low gear and blended in with traffic.

Dub and Oga sat down and reloaded their weapons. “I think we lost them,” Dub said.

As soon as they cleared the smog, they saw a police chopper fly passed them. It swirled around in midair and hover. A sniper set aim and fired. Damar heard a window shatter. Boo Boo looked in the back seat. Dub-Sac was splattered with blood. Dub and Boo Boo turned to Oga, he was slumped over with a large exit wound in the back of his head.

Boo Boo faced Damar “They got Oga!” He yelled.

The sniper fired a second shot and hit Damar in the thigh as the car flew under it. “Oh muthafucka!” Damar screamed as blood quickly soaked his pants. He had to block the pain out and keep moving. He glanced in his rearview and saw that the squad cars were back on his trail and so was the news chopper.

The sniper in the police chopper fired again, this time the bullet penetrated the roof and struck Big Boo Boo in the shoulder.

“Ahhh! You muthafuckas.” Boo Boo shouted. The pain amplified his adrenaline, he leaned out the window and unloaded his whole clip at the chopper. “Ahhhhhhhh!”

Boc! Boc! Boc! Boc!

The sniper fell away from his gun stand. “Got yo bitch ass!” Boo Boo put another cartridge in his Glock.

Dub-Sac was still bustin' at the cars behind them.

Damar was going so fast he didn't see the sign that said *Draw Bridge* up ahead. By the time he got to the toll, they were raising the bridge to prevent them from crossing. He couldn't make a U-turn because the cops were too close behind, like bees to a honeycomb. "I'ma jump this muthafucka," Damar yelled and kicked the car into third gear.

The car skipped when it hit the bridge break. The powerful engine roared as the car escalated up the rising draw bridge. Boo Boo and Dub-Sac quickly fastened their seatbelts. By the time the car reached the top, the bridge had opened up. Damar's fate laid between a forty foot gap above water. But he was determined to make the jump. He gripped the steering wheel with both hands when the car flew through the air.

Big Boo Boo braced the dashboard. "Oooh shiiiit!"

To Damar it felt like they were flying in slow motion until the car landed on the other side of the bridge. The hard impact jarred the front suspension. Damar shifted the car in neutral to calm the momentum. Once he regained control of the wheel, he snatched the car in second gear and then third, in eight seconds he was at 90 mph.

It was a quarter of a mile til the end of the bridge, Damar had lost the squad cars, but the news chopper was still there. Suddenly, the undercarriage broke and the car started sliding toward the side of the bridge.

"Hold on!" Damar yelled over the squealing tires. He jerked the wheel and the car started flipping. Right then,

Damar had flashes of his traumatic past from where it first started up until now. He saw himself holding his dying brother.

"Hang on, big bruh, hang on. You better not die on me. Somebody help!"

Then his mind flipped to another sad episode in his life. The last time he saw his sister in the trailer park.

"C'mon sis, I need you to be strong and get off the dope, you better than that and you know it. I'ma take you outta here."

"I can't, Damar. You listen to me. From this day on, don't you ever worry about somebody who don't give a damn about themselves ever again."

Suddenly the faces of all the people he killed flashed through his mind one by one, like a slide show. Then his marriage proposal to Jamerica flashed through his mind.

"Yes, yes, yes, Damar I'll marry you. But wait I have a surprise for you, too."

"What is it, baby?"

"We having a baby. We having a baby!"

"Oh, man, I'm finna be a daddy? My baby is having a baby?"

"Baby, you alright?"

"Yeah. Damn, I'm finna have a junior."

"Who said it was a boy?"

"I'm just trying to speak it in to existence. But on the real, I just pray for a healthy baby, a happy marriage and that nothing come between us. And may God forgive me for all my sins."

On the forth tumble Damar's flashbacks went poof like a cloud of smoke and he was ejected clean through the windshield. He flew over the bridge and plunged into the ocean. The car flipped three more times and landed on its roof. The Camaro slid twenty five yards before it stopped in the middle of the highway. It was still drizzling.

Boo Boo was upside down in the car barely conscious. He had a concussion and minor scratches on his face, arms and legs. He could hear the news chopper over them and the police sirens on the other side of the bridge. He smelled gas and quickly unfastened his seat belt and crawled out of the car. He slowly staggered to his feet and leaned up against the car. His right leg had a piece of metal sticking straight through it. He grabbed it with his good arm and took a deep breath and yanked it clean out of his leg and dropped it on the ground. Then he heard someone groaning inside of the car. He dropped to one knee. “Damar! Damar! Dub! Dub!”

A couple of seconds later, Dub came crawling from the wreckage. His hand and face was bloody. Boo Boo reached down and pulled him up. Then he turned back to the car and called Damar again. “Damar! Damar!”

Dub-Sac tapped him on the shoulder. “He ain’t in there.”

Boo Boo looked around with fear in his eyes. “He gotta be out here somewhere.” He may be unconscious. We gotta find him, Dub.”

Dub pointed up at the news chopper. “Well, we better hurry the police will be here in a minute.”

Dub took off one way and Boo Boo limped the other way in search of Damar. They could hear the emotional distress in each other’s voices as they called out Damar’s name.

But the possibility that Damar might be dead affected Dub-Sac more than Boo Boo because it was his drug addiction that caused all of this.

After searching the entire area where the wreck took place, Dub and Boo Boo walked over to the bridge and looked into the waving ocean. All they saw was rain and a few boat lights.

Boo Boo glanced up at the news chopper, then he looked at Dub with sadness etched across his face. “He gone, Dub.”

Dub shook his head. “Nah, my nigga, I don’t believe it.”

Suddenly they heard police sirens. They spun around and saw blue lights coming from the other end of the Turnpike.

There was nowhere to run unless they jumped into the cold ocean.

"We'll never see daylight again, Dub. Never," Boo Boo said as his eyes started to water.

Dub narrowed his eyes at Boo Boo, "I ain't going to prison." Then he ran to the Camaro.

He crawled inside and found two of their guns. When he got out of the car and stood, Boo Boo was there in front of him with his hand out.

"I ain't going either."

Dub slowly handed him one of the guns. They cocked them and looked at each other.

By this time the police had formed a barricade, there was twenty high powered riffles pointed in their direction. An officer came over the bull horn, *"Put your hands on top of your head and get down on the ground! I repeat—"*

Dub saw a tear roll down Boo Boo's face and this made one roll down his. Dub wiped his face with the back of his hand and told his best friend in the whole world, "We gonna be alright. It's a heaven for gangsta's, too, my nigga."

Boo Boo nodded then he reached in his pocket and pulled out Sandy's engagement ring. He open the box and took the ring out. He looked at it one last time and brought it to his mouth closed his eyes and kissed it. Then he turned and threw the ring in the ocean. He then looked at Dub-Sac. "If there's a heaven for us, I'm ready to go."

Dub nodded, then they turned to the road block and started shooting.

***

7 a.m. Breaking News Live on CNN.

Hi, I'm Tracy Hamilton with CNN News. I'm standing here on The New Jersey Turnpike where a high speed chase and a shootout with the local authorities ended the lives of three African Americans last night. The suspects were wanted for murdering three security guards at Riley's Pub.

A fourth suspect was thrown from the vehicle and into the ocean. The body has not been found yet. But as you can see, the divers are still searching...

Dub-Sac 1984-2015

Big Boo Boo 1982 – 2015

Oga 1980 – 2015

Damar King 1984 - ?

Flash back...
April 13, 2014 Atlanta GA.
The first meeting of The King Cartel.

"What you see here is the new King Cartel. We're only six deep right now, but I'd rather have a little of something then a lot of nothing. First, I know all of y'all know how to slang dope, but running a cartel is different. Tonight, I'm about to school you on how it's done. Most cartels deal only with family because it makes snitching near impossible and it puts the boss at a lower risk of getting knocked off. But in this case, you all are my family. We been through the trenches together since grade school. We sold dope on the same block in some of the coldest winters and hottest summers. And through all that, we never let a nigga or a bitch come between us. So, I know the type of niggas I'm putting behind me...

"Now before I go any further, I want you all to swear under The Cartel's new oath, to insure your loyalty and your dedication to the cartel...

"From this day forth, I swear to honor and respect thy brethren. No matter what comes my way, I will remain loyal to the end. Though I will be judged and tested, neither love

nor war will turn me against my brother and may nothing separate us but God."

The End

Letter to my fans

Dear fans,

I want to thank each and every one of you from the stem of my heart and soul for your precious time and caring support because without you there would be no me in this literary world. This has been a challenging journey, but it was well worth it. Along the way, I developed a deeper passion for writing and entertaining people. But I also got to meet some good people from all around the globe. It's a beautiful thing to be able to share my gift of writing. It's amazing how God works. Just 3 years ago, I never dreamed of becoming an author. That was not in my plans but they were in God's and he knows best. So I'll write until I can't write anymore. In doing so, I will strive to be the best author and friend I can be.

Yours truly,
Frank Gresham

Stay Connected with Us!

Text **LOCKDOWN** to 22828 to stay up-to-date with new releases, sneak peaks, contests and more…

Thank you!

Submission Guideline.

Submit the first three chapters of your completed manuscript to ldpsubmissions@gmail.com, subject line: Your book's title. The manuscript must be in a .doc file and sent as an attachment. Document should be in Times New Roman, double spaced and in size 12 font. Also, provide your synopsis and full contact information. If sending multiple submissions, they must each be in a separate email.

Have a story but no way to send it electronically? You can still submit to LDP/Ca$h Presents. Send in the first three chapters, written or typed, of your completed manuscript to:

LDP: Submissions Dept
Po Box 870494
Mesquite, Tx 75187

DO NOT send original manuscript. Must be a duplicate.

Provide your synopsis and a cover letter containing your full contact information.

Thanks for considering LDP and Ca$h Presents.

Coming Soon from Lock Down Publications/Ca$h Presents

BOW DOWN TO MY GANGSTA

By **Ca$h**

TORN BETWEEN TWO

By **Coffee**

BLOOD STAINS OF A SHOTTA **II**

By **Jamaica**

WHEN THE STREETS CLAP BACK **II**

By **Jibril Williams**

STEADY MOBBIN

By **Marcellus Allen**

BLOOD OF A BOSS **V**

By **Askari**

BRIDE OF A HUSTLA **III**

By **Destiny Skai**

WHEN A GOOD GIRL GOES BAD **II**

By **Adrienne**

LOVE & CHASIN' PAPER **II**

By **Qay Crockett**

THE HEART OF A GANGSTA **III**

By **Jerry Jackson**

LOYAL TO THE GAME **IV**

By **T.J. & Jelissa**

A DOPEBOY'S PRAYER **II**

By **Eddie "Wolf" Lee**

IF LOVING YOU IS WRONG… **III**

By **Jelissa**

BLOODY COMMAS **III**

SKI MASK CARTEL II

By **T.J. Edwards**

BLAST FOR ME **II**

RAISED AS A GOON V

BRED BY THE SLUMS

By **Ghost**

A DISTINGUISHED THUG STOLE MY HEART **III**

By **Meesha**

ADDICTIED TO THE DRAMA **II**

By **Jamila Mathis**

LIPSTICK KILLAH II

By **Mimi**

THE BOSSMAN'S DAUGHTERS 4

By **Aryanna**

Available Now

RESTRAINING ORDER **I & II**

By **CA$H & Coffee**

LOVE KNOWS NO BOUNDARIES **I II & III**

By **Coffee**

RAISED AS A GOON I, II, III & IV

By **Ghost**

LAY IT DOWN **I & II**

LAST OF A DYING BREED

BLOOD STAINS OF A SHOTTA

By **Jamaica**

LOYAL TO THE GAME

LOYAL TO THE GAME II

LOYAL TO THE GAME III

By **TJ & Jelissa**

BLOODY COMMAS I & II

SKI MASK CARTEL

By **T.J. Edwards**

IF LOVING HIM IS WRONG…I & II

By **Jelissa**

WHEN THE STREETS CLAP BACK

By **Jibril Williams**

A DISTINGUISHED THUG STOLE MY HEART I & II

By **Meesha**

PUSH IT TO THE LIMIT

By **Bre' Hayes**

BLOOD OF A BOSS **I, II, III & IV**

By **Askari**

THE STREETS BLEED MURDER **I, II & III**

THE HEART OF A GANGSTA I & II

By **Jerry Jackson**

CUM FOR ME

CUM FOR ME 2

CUM FOR ME 3

An **LDP Erotica Collaboration**

BRIDE OF A HUSTLA **I & II**

THE FETTI GIRLS **I, II& III**

By **Destiny Skai**

WHEN A GOOD GIRL GOES BAD

By **Adrienne**

A GANGSTER'S REVENGE **I II III & IV**

THE BOSS MAN'S DAUGHTERS

THE BOSS MAN'S DAUGHTERS II

THE BOSSMAN'S DAUGHTERS III

A SAVAGE LOVE **I & II**

BAE BELONGS TO ME

A HUSTLER'S DECEIT I, II

By **Aryanna**

A KINGPIN'S AMBITON

A KINGPIN'S AMBITION **II**

I MURDER FOR THE DOUGH

By **Ambitious**

TRUE SAVAGE

TRUE SAVAGE II

TRUE SAVAGE **III**

By **Chris Green**

A DOPEBOY'S PRAYER

By **Eddie "Wolf" Lee**

THE KING CARTEL **I, II & III**

By **Frank Gresham**

THESE NIGGAS AIN'T LOYAL **I, II & III**

By **Nikki Tee**

GANGSTA SHYT **I II &III**

By **CATO**

THE ULTIMATE BETRAYAL

By **Phoenix**

BOSS'N UP **I , II & III**

By **Royal Nicole**

I LOVE YOU TO DEATH

By Destiny J

I RIDE FOR MY HITTA

I STILL RIDE FOR MY HITTA

By **Misty Holt**

LOVE & CHASIN' PAPER

By **Qay Crockett**

TO DIE IN VAIN

By **ASAD**

BROOKLYN HUSTLAZ

By **Boogsy Morina**

BROOKLYN ON LOCK I & II

By **Sonovia**

GANGSTA CITY

By **Teddy Duke**

A DRUG KING AND HIS DIAMOND

A DOPEMAN'S RICHES

By Nicole Goosby

BOOKS BY LDP'S CEO, CA$H

TRUST IN NO MAN

TRUST IN NO MAN 2

TRUST IN NO MAN 3

BONDED BY BLOOD

SHORTY GOT A THUG

THUGS CRY

THUGS CRY 2

THUGS CRY 3

TRUST NO BITCH

TRUST NO BITCH 2

TRUST NO BITCH 3

TIL MY CASKET DROPS

RESTRAINING ORDER

RESTRAINING ORDER 2

IN LOVE WITH A CONVICT

Coming Soon

BONDED BY BLOOD 2

BOW DOWN TO MY GANGSTA

www.ingramcontent.com/pod-product-compliance
Lightning Source LLC
Chambersburg PA
CBHW070046260626
47159CB00005B/2133

* 9 7 8 1 9 4 8 8 7 8 2 3 4 *